The Fljotsdale Saga, which may perhaps be called 'the last of the sagas', is one of the forty or so Family Sagas or Sagas of Icelanders. These sagas were based to a considerable extent on oral tradition and consisted of stories about real or fictitious persons who lived in the period from the settlement of Iceland in the late ninth century to the middle of the eleventh century. The Fljotsdale Saga, which is episodic in form and intended as a *skaldsaga* or story to entertain, recounts, among other things, some of the exploits of two brothers, the Droplaugarsons. The work dates from about 1500. The author probably came from the East Fiords.

The Droplaugarsons completes the story of the brothers Grim and Helgi and is akin to the classical Family Saga. It probably dates from the early thirteenth century and is very likely the work of an inhabitant of Fljotsdale.

Dr Jean Young, who gained her MA and PhD at Cambridge, was formerly Reader in English Language and Literature at the University of Reading. Eleanor Haworth (née Arkwright) gained her MA at Cambridge.

The Fljotsdale Saga
and
The Droplaugarsons

Translated from the Icelandic by Jean Young and Eleanor Haworth
and introduced by Jean Young

J. M. Dent & Sons Ltd
EVERYMAN'S LIBRARY

© Introduction, Translation and editorial matter,
J. M. Dent & Sons Ltd, 1990

This book is set in 10 on 12 pt Sabon
by Deltatype, Ellesmere Port, S. Wirral
Made in Great Britain by the Guernsey Press Co.
Ltd, Guernsey C.I. for
J. M. Dent & Sons Ltd
91 Clapham High Street, London SW4 7TA

First published in Everyman's Library, 1990

ISBN 0460 87004.1

CONTENTS

Contents

NOTE ON THE TRANSLATIONS

These translations are based on the standard editions of *The Fljotsdale Saga* and *The Droplaugarsons* in *Islenzk Fornrit*, vol. XI (1950).

In translating compounded Icelandic place-names we have followed the example of the Penguin Classics Icelandic translations, using -by, -dale, -fiord, -heath, -hill, -ness, -river, -stead, -fell.

Apart from dropping the nominatival ending of strong nouns, e.g., Thorstein for Thorsteinn, we have not changed personal names unless they are well known, e.g., Ronald for Rognvaldr. We translate the letters 'thorn' and 'eth' as th and d respectively, and have dropped all accents.

The verses in the sagas have been translated freely into prose as it is impossible to imitate their extremely intricate verse form. However, three examples from *The Droplaugarsons*, in Chapter XIII, Nos 3, 5 and 6, indicating the Icelandic word order and meaning, are given after the rendering which makes sense.

We have provided a list of the chief characters in the sagas and, in the list of Contents, a sentence or two describing what happens in each chapter.

We wish to thank Professor Hermann Palsson for his generous help with *The Fljotsdale Saga* translation; Dr Anthony Faulkes for his with *The Droplaugarsons*, and for recommending the sagas to Dent; Pamela Holland for her professional map-making; Ann Burney for her typing; Lorraine Fletcher for photocopying; Hilda Dale for help with the proofs. Ursula Dronke for encouragement; Jocelyn Burton and her colleagues for accepting both sagas for Dent; and, of course, Judith Harte for careful editing.

Jean Young
Eleanor Haworth

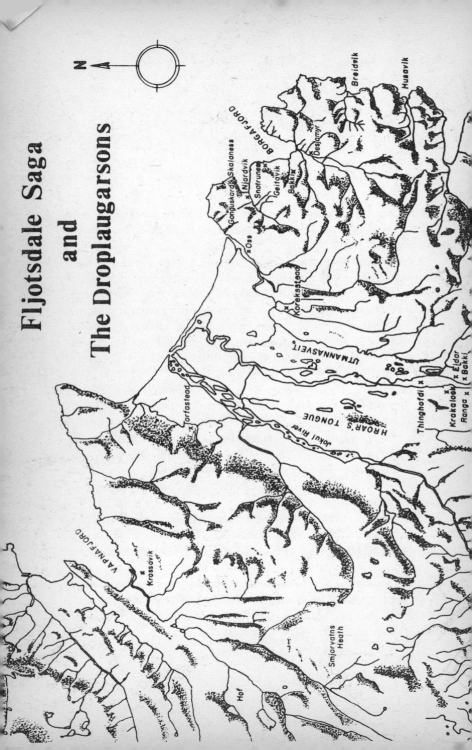

Fljotsdale Saga
and
The Droplaugarsons

INTRODUCTION

The story that has come to be known as *The Fljotsdale Saga* may perhaps be called 'the last of the sagas', that is of those tales usually designated as Family Sagas or Sagas of Icelanders. These, in number about forty, are stories about real or fictitious persons who lived in the period dating from the settlement of Iceland in the late ninth century to the mid-eleventh. They were based to a considerable extent on oral tradition and were written down some of them as early as the thirteenth century. That story-telling was a popular entertainment at the annual parliament, Althing,[1] in Iceland as early as the time of Harald Hardrada (1047–66), is indicated by reference to it in his saga. There we are told that a young Icelander once entertained his court with stories during the winter but that, at Christmas time, he became rather depressed. The king guessed that this was because he had exhausted his stock of tales. The Icelander agreed, but said he knew one more saga he did not dare to recite, because it was the story of the king's adventures abroad. The king remarked that that was just the story he most wanted to hear. When the tale was finished, he asked the Icelander where he had obtained the material for it and who had taught him the saga. He answered that every summer he used to go to the Althing and that each summer he had learned part of the story from Halldor Snorrason.

The sagas themselves, although each really needs to be considered on its own, are generally regarded as falling into various groups according to their content and style and may be

[1] The General Assembly, founded in 930, attended by freeholding farmers as well as chieftains every summer for two weeks late in June.

dated roughly as follows. The first to be written down were, like much of the twelfth-century historian Ari's *Book of Icelanders,* about ecclesiastics and the kings of Norway. Then come the Family Sagas or Sagas of Icelanders. Later are those about persons who flourished before the colonization of Iceland but who were often, or were said to be, related in some way to the settlers; and finally those about knights and ladies of medieval chivalry, these being frequently translated from foreign originals. Besides these longer narratives there are extant a number of short stories. In all these types of narrative, legendary material occurs and this forms the mainstay of the entirely fictitious tales known as 'lying sagas'. Of all these stories the Family Sagas are the best known and that deservedly so from the standpoint of characterization and style. Among them are stories about Egil, Njal, Gisli and Grettir and those about the people of Laxdale and Eyr. Our tale does not belong in this category although it recounts among other things some of the exploits of two brothers, the Droplaugarsons, who are the protagonists in the saga bearing their name, a tale artistically far closer than *The Fljotsdale Saga* to the classical saga and belonging to a radically different period.

Now in the opinion of some scholars it is incorrect to speak of a separate *Fljotsdale Saga,* since it has in MS form neither beginning nor end. It is, in the MS in which it is found, tacked on to a longer version of Hrafnkel's Saga, and since one of its main characters, Helgi Asbjarnarson, is the grandson of Hrafnkel, it may be that it was regarded by its author as a kind of sequel to that story though of later date, round about 1500. By that time the classical Family Saga was a memory only. Persons like the wise Njal, the wily Snorri, the forceful Gudrun or steadfast Bergthora belonged to the far-away past. What had inspired these stories was the sense of achievement and pride in colonizing an unknown land and building in that country with, to quote B.S. Phillpotts,[1] 'its fortuitous collections of individuals segregated into small communities by mountains, by unnavigable rivers, by deserts of sand and lava – a republic with one code of laws and one central legislative and judicial assembly held annually at a fixed time and place – institutions far in advance of custom and practice in the

[1] B. S. Phillpotts: *Edda and Saga* (1931) p. 154.

greater part of Europe'. The men of that period entertained a healthy respect for their individual identity and a sense of purposefulness in life as a people: they were democratic aristocrats. So we have from an early date, only a century after the conclusion of the settlement, the historian Ari Thorgilsson's *Islendingabok* or *Book of Icelanders*, and this was written in the vernacular. This little book gives an account of the history of the colony from about 870 to 1118 based on oral information for which the author quotes his sources. This book was followed in the early thirteenth century by the larger compilation known as *Landnamabok* or *Book of Settlements* which gives not only the names of some 400 important persons and the places they lived in, where they came from, their marriages and descendants, but short episodes which some scholars regard as containing the germ of some of the later sagas. By 1500, however, Iceland differed greatly from the country of the earlier centuries. For one thing it had ceased to be independent politically; it was much poorer and had suffered catastrophes like that of the Black Death which had devastated the population during the previous century, and had endured volcanic eruptions, pestilence and famine. It is hardly surprising, therefore, that the *Fljotsdale* story in both style and content differs somewhat from the classical Icelandic saga. Episodic in form it begins with a fantastic account of Thorvald Thidrandason's winning of Droplaug, a daughter of Bjorgolf who is called Earl of Shetland – a region that was never a separate earldom from Orkney. After this yarn in which Thorvald defeats a gigantic troll who had stolen Droplaug from her father and kept her as his mistress, there are two main stories. One relates the way in which two brothers, sons of the widow Droplaug, avenge the slandering of their mother by an unpleasant character, Thorgrim Dungbeetle. The other and longer tells us about the killing of Thidrandi Geitisson, Ketil Thrym's nephew, at the hands of a Norwegian called Gunnar – and focuses our interest on the subsequent adventures of Gunnar. This portion includes his successful bid for shelter from Sveinung, an episode exceedingly well narrated. Now these two main stories are but loosely connected and the characterization on the whole somewhat superficial. We look in vain for the overwhelming sense of fate and man's heroic struggle to resist this – Njal's conflict: the supernatural plays no part as contrasted with the way this makes for unity of atmosphere in another episodic tale, *Eyrbyggja Saga:* the dialogue on the whole lacks the bite of the quick retort; the humour is crude, witness the Droplaug brothers' treatment of Bersi's servants; erotic interest is negligible, it is just touched on for example in the account of Helgi Droplaugarson's love for Helga. More important than all these things, the individual men and women in *The Fljotsdale Saga* do not stand out as vividly as they do in the older stories; they seem in the main to be 'seen from the outside', seldom revealing themselves in speech or action: Thidrandi Geitisson scarcely indicates by his behaviour why he was looked upon as 'one of the four most accomplished men in all Iceland', although we can understand why he was greatly loved when we read the account of his conflict with his uncle Ketil Thrym.

On the other hand Helgi Asbjarnarson's father shows us what sort of person he was by the reference to him in the brief Olvid episode. Droplaug's sons are sharply differentiated: Helgi, red-haired and with a strikingly ugly mouth, is impetuous and violent. Grim, who has the fair colouring and curly hair of the tradition-ally acceptable hero, is gentler and more thoughtful, particularly when he reminds his brother of what their foster-father Bersi has done for them when Helgi wants to torment Bersi's men – we remember too that Bersi had shown favouritism to Helgi. The boys' close attachment to each other is stressed when Bersi offers at first to foster only Helgi; the latter refuses to accept unless Grim is adopted as well. In all his dealings with Helgi, Bersi reveals himself as tolerant and fair-minded, deserving his epithet 'the Wise'. Then Thordis Todda is unmistakable; after her marriage with Helgi Asbjarnarson she so totally rejects the pinch-penny life she led with her brother that she has later to regret her hospitality to all and sundry. A further aspect of this woman's nature is given us in the account of her loyalty to her husband Helgi, both in her generous adoption of his illegitimate daughter and her refusal to give Gunnar Thidrandi-killer up to her brother. Even such a minor character as the skunk Nollar is observed with some amusement when he declines to join his brother's avengers on the grounds that he is tired, has a lot to do and lives alone. And the elderly Hreidar who stays in bed till midday and sits up at night reading (anachronistically) an 'ancient saga' is unforgettable.

There is, too, something of the tragic irony so characteristic of the classical saga in the circumstance that Ketil Thrym, who considers his nephew Thidrandi the only one of his kinsfolk he would like to be on good terms with, should be killed by that same nephew. Again Gunnstein, the instigator of the unnecessary fight at Njardvik, is the sole survivor of that battle.

Further, though episodic in form and betraying, like the beginning and ending of *Droplaugarsonasaga* or *The Droplaugarsons,* the influence of the later legendary sagas, some of even the minor episodes make very good reading, for example the brief story of Olvid and the horses; and the tale of Thorgrim Dungbeetle and his brother Nollar is related with more zest than it is in *The Droplaugarsons*. It is interesting too to compare the comment made by the brothers' aunt, Groa – 'You, my nephew, have taken early to killing' – with what she is made to say at much greater length in *The Droplaugarsons;* and some readers may think that *Fljotsdale's* 'one night Grim felt a touch on his legs; it was bright moonlight' an improvement on 'They got up early', when the brothers were going out to tackle Thorgrim Dungbeetle. Above all, the adventures of Gunnar Thidrandi-killer are related in a much more stirring way than they are in the short story about him, and he receives just a brief mention in *The Droplaugarsons.*

It should be noted too that our saga throws light on the manners and customs during a period as remote from its author's lifetime as ours is from his. Thus in Chapter XI we learn about housing arrangements: 'In former times there were few "bath-rooms" in the houses.[1] Instead, in the evening big fires were made at which people could bask; there was plenty of good firewood because every district was well wooded. The houses were so arranged that each building stood end on to another, and the rooms were narrow; the hall where people sat at mealtimes was where they slept, each in his own place, when the tables were taken up. Further within the hall were closet-beds where the most

---

[1] The saga people bathed in hot springs. The word 'bathroom' came to mean 'sitting room' only later.

important men slept.' We are also told how the Droplaugarsons were dressed: 'Their everyday clothes were russet homespun tunics and breeks with a cloak and hood for outer garment.' In Chapter XVI we hear how Ketil snatched up a woollen tunic and put it on: 'before that he was wearing only footless trews, strapped under his feet, as no one wore linen breeks at that time'. In Chapter XIX we are told how they carried their knives: 'In those days no one wore a knife in his belt; when men went out they had a knife hanging on a strap round the neck.'

Passages relating to the daily life and occupations of the farmer run throughout the narrative and are exceedingly well told; the saga as a whole gives us a realistic picture of what it was like to live in Iceland centuries ago.

We know little about the authors of the Icelandic sagas; it is usually impossible to assign any specific example to any given informant and this is the case with *The Fljotsdale Saga*. But it would appear from the writer's familiarity with persons and places in the East Fiords of the country that he came from that district. He was certainly well read in sagas and short stories emanating from these parts: those about Thorstein the White, the men of Weaponfiord, Hrafnkel, the Droplaugarsons, Brand-Krossi, Gunnar Thidrandi-killer. It was undoubtedly *The Droplaugarsons* that inspired him to write about the brothers Grim and Helgi. From the other stories he seems merely to have borrowed a name or nickname as the case might be. He appears also to have been acquainted with the tales about Njal, the Laxdalers, Hallfred and the Ljosvetnings, stories belonging to other regions of Iceland.

We may gather from his interest in the ways of his ancestors that our author was something of an antiquarian and it is perhaps worth noting that he occasionally models his style on that of the older sagas when he uses phrases like 'It is said' or 'It was said', which he does no fewer than sixteen times in twenty-six chapters. And something of his personality may be gleaned from his attitude to his characters. He probably resembled the tolerant Bersi. That he was a man of peace is indicated by the way he makes Grim reproach his brother Helgi for his violent wrecking of Bersi's temple and, as already noted, he lays great stress on the good relationship between the brothers. He admired physical courage and prowess, witness his account of Gunnar's escape from his pursuers. It is clear too that he considered Gunnar a victim of chance so that, in spite of his killing of Thidrandi whose death was mourned by many (it killed his foster-father Hroar), he engages our sympathy. It has already been noted that he appreciates even his 'baddies', and it is possible, from the remarks of some of these, to surmise he felt a different attitude to chieftains from that expressed at the end of Chapter II – perhaps Asbjorn's remark does not really meet with his approval? From the zest with which he unfailingly invests his tale it is certain that he enjoyed his story-telling and it is therefore hoped that modern readers of the present translation may discover some pleasure in perusing it. *The Fljotsdale Saga* deserves to be read for what it was intended to be: a *skaldsaga,* that is a story to entertain.

A translation of the little *Droplaugarsonasaga* is included in the present work because it completes the story of the two brothers Grim and Helgi, which in *The Fljotsdale Saga* ends abruptly with Helgi's wrecking of the gods in his foster-father Bersi's heathen temple. The *Droplaugarsonasaga* begins and ends with palpably legendary material and has come down to us in a much mutilated state from, probably, the early thirteenth century. Nevertheless, it is akin to the classical Family Saga and this is most apparent in two passages: one is the brilliant description of the fight in Eyvindardale in which Helgi meets his end, and the other, the memorable one in which Grim avenges his brother's death. And there is one unusual thing to note about this saga. If its last words are not merely added to inspire belief in the story, the *Droplaugarsonasaga* is the only Icelandic saga to which an author has been assigned – namely the great-grandson of Grim Droplaugarson himself. The colophon runs: After Ingjald's death Helga [Grim's widow] lived on at Arneidarstead with their son Thorkel. Thorvald had a son Ingjald. His son was called Thorvald who told this story. Helgi Droplaugarson fell the year after Thangbrand came to Iceland [i.e. 997 or 998].

This colophon may be genuine, although it looks as if the scribe has confused the names Thorkel and the first-named Thorvald. This does not, however, invalidate the idea that a descendant of

Grim's told the tale. In any case the written *Droplaugarsonasaga*, probably the work of an inhabitant of Fljotsdale, is unmistakably worth reading for more than the two scenes mentioned above – which exhibit Icelandic story-telling at its best.

LIST OF CHIEF CHARACTERS IN THE FLJOTSDALE SAGA

Helgi Asbjarnarson . . . . .chieftain
Olvid Oddsson of Oddsstead . . . . .a farmer
Thordis Todda . . . . .second wife of Helgi Asbjarnarson
Gudrun Osvif's daughter . . . . .wife of Thorkel Eyjolfsson
Thidrandi Geitisson . . . . .grandson of Thidrandi the Old
Ketil Thrym . . . . .son of Thidrandi Geitisson of Njardvik
Bjorgolf . . . . .Earl of Shetland
Asbjorn Wall-hammer . . . . .builder for Ketil Thidrandason
Gunnar . . . . .a Norwegian
Sveinung . . . . .a farmer
Droplaug .Bjorgolf's daughter
Thorvald Thidrandason . . . . .Droplaug's first husband
Helgi and Grim . . . . .sons of Droplaug
Bersi the Wise . . . . .foster-father of the Droplaugarsons and owner of a heathen temple
Groa . . . . .sister of Droplaug
Thorir of Myness . . . . .a farmer
Thorgrim Dungbeetle . . . . .slanderer of Droplaug
Nollar . . . . .brother of Thorgrim Dungbeetle
Hallstein . . . . .second husband of Droplaug

CHIEF CHARACTERS NOT IN THE FLJOTSDALE SAGA, BUT IN THE DROPLAUGARSONASAGA

Droplaug Grimsdottir .... mother of Helgi and Grim

Hrafnkel Thorisson .... chieftain and later Godi

Ozur of Ass .... farmer

Holmstein Bersason of Vidivellir. . . farmer

Geitir Lytingsson of Krossavik. .... farmer

Thord of Geirolfseyr .... farmer

Bjorn of Snotruness .... farmer

Thorgrim Furcap of Midboer ..... farmer

Thorkel Geitisson of Krossavik ... farmer

Thorkel Black Poet .... friend of Helgi Droplaugar-son

Gaus .... a (berserk) viking

THE FLJOTSDALE SAGA

I

There was a woman called Thorgerd who lived in the east, in Fljotsdale; she was a widow and though of very good family, she was short of money at that time. She lived at the place now called Thorgerdarstead.

Thorir Hrafnkelsson's kinsmen wanted him to settle down; they urged him to ask for Thorgerd's hand, saying that this match would help to establish his position. Thorir got her, and the marriage feast was to be at Hrafnkelsstead in a month's time; his brother Asbjorn was invited to the feast.

A man called Glum lived on the west side of Fljotsdale at a place now called Glumsstead. His wife Thurid was the daughter of Hamund, and she came from a Thjorsardale family in the south; they had one daughter called Oddbjorg. Early one morning mother and daughter went to the cowshed. The herdsman was there, but Glum was lying in his bed. When the women came back to the house it had been overwhelmed by a landslide; Glum and the entire household had perished there, except for these three people. After this event Thurid moved across the river, rather higher up than before; there she lived a long time, and that farm is now called Thuridarstead. This news reached Hrafnkelsdale. Thurid was a very knowledgeable woman and an outstanding person, and brought up her daughter with great care; the girl was also very beautiful and most accomplished.

When Asbjorn got his brother's wedding invitation he welcomed it, and called his friends together. He rode eastwards over the heath to Thuridarstead with this purpose, to ask for the hand of Oddbjorg. This was agreed, and he then rode down to the feast taking his bride-to-be with him. The feast went off well and a big crowd of people were there. After it was over Asbjorn rode home with his wife west over the heath to Adalbol. They got on well together.

Thorir and Thorgerd lived together and had a son called Hrafnkel and a daughter called Eyvor; she was married to Hakon of Hakonsstead who settled in Jokulsdale. Asbjorn and Oddbjorg had four daughters who all died in infancy, but at last they had a son called Helgi who grew up at home and was a most promising man. The cousins Hrafnkel and Helgi grew up together in the district, though there was four years' difference between them. The brothers Thorir and Asbjorn held their position for a long time, and the families were on good terms as long as both were alive. Thorir died of sickness, and afterwards his widow, together with his young son Hrafnkel, took over the property and authority under Asbjorn's guidance. Helgi grew up at Adalbol with his father, and was thought to excel other men in every way, both in good looks and in disposition.

A man called Odd had settled in the neighbourhood, and he was both blind and old at that time. He had a son called Olvid, who took over the management of his father's affairs. Olvid was a very big man, the most garrulous of men, and much disliked for being indiscreet, stupid and ill-natured; he was also most unjust in every way. All the same he provided well for his household, both from the fiords below him and the fells above.

II

One summer it happened that Olvid made ready to go into the Fljotsdale district, right up to the glaciers to collect moss, and on this journey he and his men let their horses stray down into Fljotsdale. They searched for them all across the heath, but could not find them. When they came to the head of Hrafnkelsdale they saw a great number of Asbjorn's stud-horses down in the valley, and Olvid told his men to seize them and put his loads on them. The men thought it would not be wise to take horses belonging to

Asbjorn: 'his father never lets anyone get away with that sort of thing,' they said.[1]

Olvid said he did not mean to be stranded up on the fells while there were horses for the taking. 'And I don't care whose they are; I'm going to make free with those horses.' So they took them, and laid packs on them, and went home with them to Oddsstead.

Afterwards Olvid sent the horses west over the heath, and they were in a filthy state. When they had come back, Asbjorn rode east over the heath and came to Oddsstead. He knocked on the door and called to Olvid to come out; he came out and welcomed Asbjorn. Asbjorn asked Olvid what compensation he was going to pay for this offence, but Olvid said he owed him nothing.

'As far as I know,' said Asbjorn, 'I've never harmed anyone, and I won't make too much of this if you'll allow others to fix fair compensation; unless you would rather we settled it between ourselves.'

Olvid said he could not see what there was to talk about, and he did not want any settlement. 'It seems obvious to me that none of us farmers should have to do without, because something we need is owned by another man; and I should say that you and I are all square, though you have more authority than I have. I'll have compensation from you in this affair before I pay any to you, or to others I may have served in the same way.'

Asbjorn said that such talk would not do him any good, and with that he rode away home where he stayed throughout the winter. Then, when the time drew on to the Spring Assembly, Asbjorn rode down into the Fljotsdale district and summoned Olvid to the Spring Assembly at Kidjafell – this meeting-place is on the ridge between Skridudale and Fljotsdale – accusing him of taking the horses. There was no one for the defence, and Asbjorn got Olvid outlawed. He then rode over to Olvid's place and held a court of execution; after that he rode to Oddsstead farm, caught Olvid in his bed, dragged him out, and killed him on the spot. Asbjorn said this was the way to deal with insignificant men who provoked important ones.

[1] In *Hrafnkel's Saga*, Hrafnkel kills his shepherd Einar for taking his horse Freyfaxi to ride without his permission.

Asbjorn divided the property between himself and Olvid's widow. She took the money and household goods, and he took the farm, and appointed a bailiff to manage it, while he himself stayed on at Adalbol for a time. And now we must turn away and leave him for the present.

III

A man called Thidrandi Ketilsson lived at the farm called Njardvik, which lies between the districts of Fljotsdale and Borgarfiord. He had authority over Njardvik, and up the district as far as the Sel river which flows west from the heath between Gilsarteig and Ormsstead, and so down into Lagarfljot.[1] It forms the northern boundary, and Lagarfljot the western, of the area known as Utmannasveit, and at that time one hundred and ninety yeomen farmed the land.

Thidrandi was a powerful man, but he was much liked all the same, for he was easy-going with his inferiors. He was a tall, strong man, and bold as a lion; he farmed for a long time and was free-handed with gifts. When he became an old man he was called Thidrandi the Old, and so indeed he was, for it is said that he was still hale and hearty at the age of a hundred and forty-six; he took good care of his livestock, and always kept an eye on matters that his workmen might neglect.

One winter, at the season when ewes are on heat, some of his men had rowed out to sea to fish, and some were fetching hay when Thidrandi went out to his ram shed in the farmyard. In the evening everyone came home but he himself, and people began to wonder where he could be. Some of the women said he had gone out to the ram shed, so they looked for him there. He was sitting outside against the shed, and they asked him why he did not come home.

He said he found it difficult to walk, and in no way easier now than before because, he said, a ram had broken his thigh-bone. So he was carried home and put to bed. After this the pain flared up and his thigh became much swollen, and that led to his death.

---

[1] This name means Lagar water; the Sel river does not flow into Lagarfljot today.

Thidrandi left two sons: Ketil was the elder and Thorvald the younger; both were big men. Thorvald was extremely handsome, quiet and not meddlesome; on the whole he was a most peaceable man. Ketil was the strongest man of his time; his looks were dark and striking, but though an ugly man, he bore himself nobly. As a rule he was very gentle, but early in his life he grew reserved and taciturn; he was called Thrum-Ketil.[1] There were great faults in his disposition and some said he had an illness. About once a fortnight it happened that a shivering fit came over him, so that every tooth chattered in his head, and he roused up out of his bed. Then great fires had to be made for him, and everything that people could think of done to relieve him. After the cold and the shuddering came a great rage, when he spared nothing before him, whether wooden walls or posts or people; he even waded through fire if it was in his way, and then drove ahead through the walls or the door-frame if they were before him, and people got out of his way if they could. So it happened every time this fit came over him, but when it left him he was mild and self-controlled. All this had a great effect on him, and on many others as he grew older.

The sister of these brothers, and the daughter of Thidrandi the Old, was called Hallkatla. She was married to Geitir Lytingsson who lived at Krossavik to the north in Vapnafiord. Geitir was a popular man and gave very great support to Hallkatla, and they got on very well together. They had two sons: the elder was called Thorkel and the younger Thidrandi after his grandfather. These brothers were both very accomplished, but different from each other. Thorkel was a dark man with reddish-brown hair; he was short but strong, and was called the smallest man of his time; however, he was very quick and active. He proved able to give a good account of himself when he had to face heavy odds, and this was not seldom.

Thidrandi Geitisson was a very big man and very strong, and more distinguished than any other man at that time. It is said that he was one of the four most accomplished men in all Iceland, the second being named as Kjartan Olafsson; the third was Hoskuld Thorgeirsson the Godi[2] of the Ljosvetnings, and the fourth Ingolf

---

[1] He is afterwards called Ketil Thrym (p. 39).
[2] Hereditary ruler of a district (godord) who was also a priest and collected the temple dues.

Thorsteinsson who was called Ingolf the Handsome.

Wise men say that no one in the whole of Iceland has been as accomplished as these four men, and this is also said of their looks, that many women lost their heads at the sight of their beauty; and by common report their other gifts did not lag behind.

IV

There was a man called Hroar. He lived on the farm called Hof which is in the Fljotsdale district west of Lagarfljot, beyond the Rang river, and east of the Jokul river. This neighbourhood takes its forename from Hroar and is called Hroar's Tongue, while he also took a name from Tongue and was called Tongue Priest. He was an old man at that time and childless, but very wealthy. It is told that Hroar made ready to leave home, and travelled north to Vapnafiord. He arrived at Outer Krossavik in the evening, and Geitir Lytingsson welcomed him warmly and invited him to stay as long as he wished. Hroar Tongue Priest stayed there for three nights, then he asked for the horses of his company to be fetched and said he would now make known his errand.

'I have come here to ask for the fostering of your son Thidrandi,' he said. 'If you agree to this, I will give him money, a place of his own, and authority after my time, but Thorkel can inherit your position after your day. I shall only consider my journey successful if you grant what I ask. We shall both find great resources of strength in this man, because he is your son, and my foster-son and heir.'

Geitir said he had no inclination to refuse so great an honour, so Thidrandi went eastwards with Hroar into Tongue, and Hroar brought him up in the best possible way.

Thidrandi had only been there a little while before everyone could see that Hroar was very fond of him, and that far beyond everyone else; indeed he was much beloved both then, and right up to the day of his death. Thidrandi was six years old when he went to his fostering at Krossavik; Thorkel was then ten years old.

V

The Njardvik brothers did not see eye to eye about money matters. Ketil wanted to decide everything himself, but Thorvald, having no say, soon got tired of this and asked to have the money and chieftainship divided between them. Ketil told him to arrange these matters as soon as he liked, and said he did not grudge him a full half of the money, 'but my chieftainship is small and I cannot bring myself to divide it. I grudge it to anyone but myself.'

Thorvald thought they both owned equal shares, though he had never had the use of his. 'I have seen for a long time', he said, 'that you want to keep me down in many ways. However, I seem to have no choice but to take such money as you scrape together for me, so we'll settle it now, although you are not treating me fairly. But you must understand that I think myself entitled to a half share of the whole, though as things are I have not got it.'

Then Ketil mustered all the valuables, and gave Thorvald a half share of everything, livestock, movable goods and everything that was indoors, except the godord, which he did not divide.

After that Thorvald went away with all his possessions to the other side of the heath, and he let out his share of the land and hired out his livestock.

A ship was laid up in Fljotsdale district in the Una estuary by the eastern fells. Thorvald went along there with his wares, took passage on the ship, and went abroad. When they stood out to sea they got contrary winds, and all summer long they tossed about here and there. When summer was over they ran into a great storm with violent winds which drove them towards land, and one night they sailed into Shetland. There was a strong ebb-tide; they got into breakers over the rocks and the ship broke in pieces. All the cargo was lost, but the men came to shore alive. Thorvald landed with the others; he was wearing Icelandic clothes. Nothing belonging to him was cast ashore except a big spear, and this he took in his hand. He stayed two days and two nights beside the sea, waiting to see if any of his goods would be washed up, but it was not to be, and nothing of his was found. Then he thought it better not to stay there any longer with nothing to eat, and when day came he went off.

At that time Shetland was ruled by an earl called Bjorgolf,[1] and he was then an old man. Thorvald thought it best to go to the earl's hall, so in the evening he waited near the door, and in the morning went before the earl. The earl was popular with his people, and yet at that time he was sad. Thorvald greeted the earl who received him well and asked who he was. He said he was an Icelander, a freedman of no great family, and now lately shipwrecked and penniless. 'Give me winter quarters, sire, for I should like to be with you.'

The earl said, 'You look to me in need of such help.'

Thorvald asked to be shown where to sit. The earl said, 'Sit on the lower bench, for slaves and freedmen sit together there. In spite of your misfortunes be quiet and as cheerful as you can.'

Thorvald went to the seat, and he stayed there for the winter. He behaved as the earl advised, being good-humoured with his bench-fellows, who indeed were easy enough in answering the questions he was forever asking them.

So the winter passed along towards Christmas time, when they all became gloomy, and the earl very sorrowful. The earl had a young wife and two sons, young in years but handsome in looks. One evening Thorvald asked those nearest to him why the men were so sad; no one would tell him, and so Christmas drew near. Then one night, the men who lay nearest Thorvald heard him cry out in his sleep. They wanted to wake him up, but the earl told them to let him dream his dream out. When he awoke they asked him what he had been dreaming, but he would not tell them. Then two nights before they celebrated Christmas, Thorvald went to the earl and greeted him respectfully. The earl replied graciously, and Thorvald said, 'I have come to ask you something that no one else will tell me. I want to know the reason why all the people here are so sad, for they are neither sleeping nor eating, and I feel some distress myself because of this. It seems to me that you are the most likely to tell me as you are their chieftain.'

The earl said he had better not ask any more. 'This matter has nothing to do with you; you cannot do anything about it, and you'll get no thanks from me for your curiosity. There are many

[1] Shetland was never an earldom in reality.

things you should not pry into, and it would be only right if someone were to pay for this.'

Thorvald said he would not have asked if he had known the earl would take it amiss. 'I'll say no more about it, but I should like to ask you to interpret my dream.'

'I am not much of a dreamer,' said the earl, 'nor can I interpret dreams. I pay no attention to them, but you may tell me yours if you want to.'

'I thought I went down towards the sea,' said Thorvald, 'and I was wearing the same clothes I put on every day. I thought it was bright enough for me to see my way. I had my spear in my hand. When I reached the sea, I thought it was ebb- and not flood-tide. I seemed to walk along by the sea where it was ebbing over wide stretches of sand, and when that ended I came to a low skerry, and went through a cleft where there was a thick growth of seaweed, and then I saw a great hill or mountain with cliffs, and a huge high precipice coming down to the sea. I thought I walked beneath the precipice until I came to shallow water under it, and I thought I waded forward until it got deep. Then I came to a shingle beach and followed it for a long time between the sea and the cliff until I saw a great cave and went inside.

'I saw a light burning so that there was no shadow anywhere, and I saw an iron pillar reaching up to the roof and a woman bound to the pillar. Her hands were tied behind her, and her hair was wound round the pillar; there were iron chains round her with a lock at one end that held her fast. I thought I tried to free her, and I managed to do this; I saw no other living thing there, but only herself. Then I took her away with me and I thought I reached the shallow water under the cliff and was wading through it, when some living creature seemed to be chasing me, and I was very much afraid. We two met together, and I do not remember how it went between us; I must have cried out in my sleep. Then I woke up.'

When the earl heard this he grew so red and swollen with such rage that one finger might have drawn blood from him.

'It is outrageous,' he said, 'that you should say you have dreamt what other men have told you; my grief is enough without my being reminded of it; how well I remembered when my daughter disappeared. It is only fitting that whoever told you should suffer, for I forbade anyone to speak of it.'

Thorvald answered, 'You must believe, sire, that none of your men have told me of these events; they were shown me in a dream, and I will only speak of them as much as you wish.'

The earl fell silent, and after a time he replied: 'One of two things must be true about you: either you have second sight or before long you will be dead.'

'I wish, sire,' said Thorvald, 'that you would tell me what has happened here in your household, for it seems to me that there is much to relate.'

'I might as well tell you,' replied the earl. 'Before my two boys I had a daughter called Droplaug. People said she was accomplished and I loved her very much. Last Christmas she disappeared. A giant called Geitir took her, and he lives where you came in your dream; the place is called Geitir's Crag and the mountain Geitir's Pillar. That monster of a man does a great deal of harm; he maims both men and beasts, and is the most evil creature in all Shetland. I have promised to give my daughter to the man, whoever he may be, who is bold enough to get her away.'

Thorvald said he thought it unlikely she could be rescued from that place.

'I would not have let her go without a dowry,' answered the earl, 'if I could have helped it. It seems to me you ought to be willing to take some risk, as you are the first one to ask about it.'

'I wish I never had asked,' said Thorvald, and he turned on his heel and went back to his seat. That evening he spoke to no one.

After supper everyone went to bed, and when he was sure they were all asleep, Thorvald got up and took his spear in his hand; he went out and down to the sea, and it was ebb-tide, and not flood. He walked northwards along some sand in much the same way as he had done in his dream. He came to the skerry, and the cleft with the thick growth of seaweed, and then the shingle beach was before him. He walked on further until he reached the shallow water under the cliff, and he waded through it; then he came to the place he had seen in his dream, and he walked up to the cave and went inside.

On one side he saw a light burning, and on the other side a bed, much larger than any he had ever seen before; he thought that if he lay down on it, and another man just as tall lay down feet to feet with him, there would still be plenty of room and Thorvald was an exceptionally tall man. This bed measured no less across than in length; it had a velvet cover over it and tapestry hangings. The feather quilts were so huge that they swelled high above the bedstead. He saw a great sword hanging over the bed, and when he took it down a lot of stones fell down too; the sword had a fine scabbard and an iron guard, but was not ornamented in any way. He drew the blade and it was green in colour, but the edges were bright, and there was no rust on it. He had never seen a weapon more worth having. At the other side of the cave he saw a stack of goods; he saw all kinds of Icelandic wares lying there, and linen cloth goods of many kinds to which he could put a name. There was also a great store of good food, and plenty of drink. All manner of good things were there that it would be better to have than to lack.

In the middle of the cave he saw an iron pillar and a woman bound to it, just as it had been in his dream. She sat there in a red gown, and beautiful as she had appeared in his dream, she now looked lovelier by far. He went up to her, and she greeted him and he replied courteously, asking her who she was.

She told him, saying she was called Droplaug, and was the daughter of Earl Bjorgolf. She asked him not to waste words, 'because you will have to try to escape with your life; you are in worse danger than you know. A troll has power here, and he is so huge that there is no other like him; also I am bound so fast that you will never get me free.'

He said he was going to take her away with him.

She said that he would not be able to, 'because the troll is greater by far than a mortal man can face. He will soon be coming home, for he goes hunting at night, and chains me to the pillar while he is away. In the daytime he lies in his bed, and amuses himself with me, picking me up and tossing me from hand to hand. When he wants to sleep he gives me gold and jewels to play with, and brings me only the food I can enjoy; he thinks he can't do enough to please me.'

'Both of us will escape,' said Thorvald, 'or neither of us.'

Then he drew the sword and hewed at her iron bonds, and struck so well that they fell apart. Then he led her out of the cave, taking no treasure with him except the sword.

They walked along the shingle as far as the shallow water under the cliff, and when he found that she was exhausted, because the giant had worn her out, he picked her up in his arms and waded through the water which was much deeper than before because it was now high tide. He looked up at the cleft in the precipice and saw that it seemed to have been hewn out with a quarrying tool, but he couldn't reach it. He saw the stars, and it was near daybreak.

He had walked a good way along the flat skerry and was finding it hard going, when he heard a loud shout from the cave behind him.

The woman was much frightened by this sound and said he must put her down, 'and I told you before you would not be able to rescue me; now save yourself. He has come home and will be wanting me; he won't search for you if he finds me.'

Thorvald answered, 'That shall never be; we shall both share the same fate as long as I can hold on to you.'

He took off his fur cloak and put it round her, and set her down in the cleft with the spear at her side, then he turned back along the way they had come. He saw the giant's head against the sky, much higher than the cliff; he carried great rocks to the woman and put them round her so that she could not get away. Then he took the sword and went to meet the giant.

The giant shouted to him to let his mistress go: 'You wretch, you are taking a lot on yourself if you think to get her away from me; I've had her a long time.' And with that the giant put one foot up on to the cleft in the precipice Thorvald had seen and trod on the skerry with the other, and his shoes were not wet, so Thorvald realized the cleft was there because the giant did not like wading. Then Thorvald sprang up under the giant who reached out with his huge hand trying to seize him. Thorvald struck at him with the sword, caught the middle of his thigh and cut off the left leg above the knee and the right one below, and the sword came down into the sand.

The giant fell down, and spoke in great pain. 'You have

deceived me utterly', he said, 'by taking the one weapon that could give me a wound. I came after you fearlessly, never thinking that a little man could bring about my death, and now you'll believe you have won a great victory, and that you and your descendants will carry that weapon; but I tell you there will come a time when it fails a man in his greatest need.'

Thorvald determined that the giant should not speak any more harmful words and struck at his neck, taking off the head. He placed the head between the thighs,[1] but he had to wait until the giant stopped flailing about with his arms and lay still, before he could do this. Then he left the giant and went up to where the woman was lying, and found that she had swooned or fainted away. He lifted her up, and she suddenly awoke as if from sleep. He carried her until they came back to the hall where men were drinking after breakfast. The people had missed Thorvald but had not thought much of it, and now he came walking into the hall with Droplaug on one arm and the sword in the other hand. He went up to the earl and greeted him, saying that he had brought him his daughter. The earl was overjoyed, and so were many others, and the earl asked him through what dangers, or by what means, he had reached her. Thorvald told him the whole story, saying it had gone much like his dream.

'You have great good fortune and you are a lucky man,' answered the earl, 'for you have conquered the worst enemy we have ever had here, and we'll soon see this for ourselves.'

The retainers said it could not be such a huge troll as people had been making out: 'That must be a lie because, after all, Thorvald has killed it by himself.'

Thorvald was turning to go back to his seat, when the earl called after him, and told him to sit on the front bench before the high-seat.

'One of two things must be true of you,' said the earl. 'Either you are worthy of more honour than I have shown you, or you will not live a long life. But everyone can see you have brought us a good gift; your adventure has turned out well, and it is still fresh in our minds that no one else would face this risk. However, we shall

---

[1] This was done to prevent the dead man's ghost from walking again.

not be able to enjoy having my daughter back until I know
without any doubt that this devil is dead.'

After that, drinking went on only for a short time, and then the
tables were taken down. Earl Bjorgolf told his men to take their
weapons and go and see what had happened. They set off, and
Thorvald with them, and they came to where the monster was
lying, and now all could see how he had been defeated; and many
of those who had called it a trifling exploit would hardly go near
him. The earl had trees felled and hauled and a pyre built. The
giant was dragged on to it and burned to cold cinders and these
were taken away and scattered out to sea. Then they went to the
cave by ship, and took away much wealth and all that was
valuable, and brought it home. Ever since then the place has been
called Geitir's Cave and Geitir's Cliff, and it is not related that
trolls have lived there again.

VI

When they got home the goods were sorted out, and it is said that
most of the cargo from Thorvald's ship was there, and that
Thorvald recognized all his own wares. Thorvald and the earl
allowed each man to take what he knew to be his own, and yet a
great deal was not claimed, for the Icelandic wares seemed
insignificant alongside the great abundance of other wealth
amassed by many men, which was found there.

Afterwards Thorvald gave splendid rewards to the men who
had been put to all this trouble.

Thorvald was now much honoured in Shetland, for he was held
to have achieved a notable exploit; the earl honoured no one
above Thorvald and others followed his lead. Thorvald stayed
there for the following year, and that same summer people in
Iceland heard of the renown he had won in Shetland. Many men
in the East Fiords were pleased when they heard of it, but not his
brother Ketil; he behaved as if he had heard nothing. People
thought that Thorvald had been very lucky, seeing how shabbily
Ketil had treated him.

Thorvald stayed in Shetland until the next Christmas and then
went to the earl and greeted him, and asked him if he remembered

anything about the Christmas before. The earl said he remembered it clearly.

'Then I claim the reward which you yourself offered when I told you my dream. You promised to give your daughter to the man who should rescue her, and now I want to know the upshot of my claim; I shall not stay on here if there is nothing to keep me.'

'I am of the same mind now as I was then,' replied the earl. 'I still think you are the man best fitted to marry her if that would give you pleasure. The match does not seem to me such a good one as it did then: the woman's disposition may not suit everyone; however, you must manage your own affairs. I will stand by everything I promised, and you will be the one to suffer if things go wrong. All the same I expect it will turn out well, as she likes you, and whenever you are mentioned, she says that no one is your equal. I will also give you the earldom until my sons are able to rule over it.'

Thorvald said he did not want that, 'because I think it would be best for you to keep it until they take over. I am not from a noble family, so it would not be fitting for me to have it.'

After that Droplaug's mother was sent for. She was called Arneid, and her brother was Grim, and their father was a Dane called Helgi and their mother was Hallerna. Arneid and Grim came there and were told of the marriage contract. They said they thought there was no one better fitted to marry this woman than this man, they gave their hearty consent and with that Droplaug was betrothed to Thorvald with a large dowry.

A fine feast was arranged, there was no lack of plentiful provisions or crowds of guests, and it was successful in every way. When it was over Thorvald gave everyone handsome presents; he grew so popular that nearly all men wished him well. He stayed there through the winter till spring came, then he bought a ship that was laid up in the Thurso river, and took his great wealth there, together with his wife Droplaug. She excelled other women both in appearance and ability and though rather haughty, reserved and arrogant with others, she and Thorvald got on well together because they cared for each other. Arneid, her mother, had many legitimate children, but she was a widow when she had her daughter, Droplaug. That spring Arneid gave her house to her sons, and married off her daughter Groa; then she made ready to take ship with Thorvald, as she wanted to go to Iceland with her daughter Droplaug. Grim Hallernuson also sailed with them. When they were ready they put to sea, and got good weather and favourable winds; they reached Iceland early in the summer.

The ship came to a place called Haven, south of Njardvik on Borgarfiord. Many of Thorvald's kinsmen rode to the ship when they heard of his arrival, and welcomed him warmly. They invited him to come and stay, urging him to bring with him as large a company as he pleased. But his brother Ketil did not come to the ship, nor did Thorvald send word to him. Ketil was married by then, and had a son whose name was Thorkel, and who was called Very Wise; there is little about him in this story, though later on he does come into it.

VII

There was a man called Hallstein who lived at Jorvik farm: he was a young man, newly married, and a near kinsman of the Njardvikings. Before Thorvald went abroad he had been a very close friend of this man who, when he heard of Thorvald's return, rode to the ship and invited him to come with his whole company and stay for the winter. Thorvald thanked him, and he and Droplaug went there with their servants, making four in all; his other shipmates were quartered further up the district. The ship was laid up and fenced round; the winter passed by and Thorvald stayed at Jorvik in great content. In the spring his kinsmen advised him to claim his godord and chieftainship from his brother Ketil, but Thorvald said he would not. 'It would be useless to do that, and my reputation would only suffer if I quarrelled with my kinsfolk.'

It is said that Thorvald set off with some companions and rode up the district and then west over Lagarfljot and all along the shore of the lake until he came to the farm called Vallholt. There was little building there, but enough land to run as a farm, and Thorvald paid down money for it; he put up more buildings and established a farmstead there, and it has been accounted a good one ever since.

After that Arneid, his mother-in-law, took over the whole indoor management of the house, and its name was changed to Arneidarstead. Thorvald settled there and soon became very popular; Droplaug did not concern herself with household affairs; she was a proud woman and people thought highly of her. As was written before, Thorvald was not the owner of a godord, and yet he was so much liked that almost everyone would sit or stand as he wished. His kinsmen sought his favour, while he himself was friendly with everyone.

A man called Bersi the son of Ozur lived in Fljotsdale west of Lagarfljot, on the farm at the head of the lake called Bersastead. He had two children, a son called Ormstein and a daughter Thorlaug; Ormstein was married and lived at South Vidivellir, but Thorlaug was young at that time. Bersi was a man of great wisdom and was called Bersi the Wise, and the farm at Bersastead was named after him. Thorvald felt great friendship for this man and Bersi for him.

Most of those who had come to Iceland with Thorvald set sail again with the ship, for he was sending it to Earl Bjorgolf loaded with Icelandic merchandise. Grim Hallernuson stayed in Iceland as he did not want to go abroad, and he bought himself the land called Gilj in the lower part of Jokulsdale. He lived there two years and then became ill and died, and his sons took over the management of the farm and property.

This first year that Thorvald and Droplaug lived at Arneidarstead, she was pregnant. Time passed until in due course she gave birth to a child, and it was a boy; he was sprinkled with water[1] and given the name of Helgi. This boy grew up at home with his father, and was a most promising lad; it was not long before another son was given to them, and he was called Grim after Grim Hallernuson. Both brothers, with two years between them, grew up full of promise.

Arneid managed the house for four years until she died; her burial mound stands above the farm and outside the fence. After that Droplaug took over the management of everything and did it well.

---

[1] This has been regarded as customary in heathen times.

VIII

There was a man called Gunnar who was closely related to the Njardvikings. He asked for the hand of a woman called Rannveig, and they were betrothed; then he made ready a feast and invited many people to it. He invited Thorvald and Droplaug, and whatever companions they wished to bring, and they promised to make the journey. When the time came to set off, Thorvald asked Droplaug if she was coming with him, but she declared that she had no intention of going, 'and I wish we could both act alike in this,' she said.

Thorvald asked her why she had changed her mind, 'for you promised, just as I did'.

'That's neither here nor there,' she replied, 'and I beg you not to go either, for my mind misgives me that we shall gain little from this feast. I am determined not to go, but I suppose you will go ahead with your journey, even though I beg you not to.'

'I could not bear to fail my kinsmen in this,' answered Thorvald, 'after we have both promised to go; but I would give up the journey if I had not pledged my word so solemnly.'

Then he made ready for his journey, but she was heavy at heart. Thorvald and nine others now went down to a ten-oared boat. He was well armed and Droplaug asked him to leave the sword behind, 'because I have a foreboding about your journey; not for the sword, that is nothing to me compared with you yourself'.

Thorvald said he took little account of people's forebodings, 'but you have never behaved like this before, and the sword does not mean so much to me that I can't do without it'.

Thorvald now came to the ship and Droplaug with him; she found it very hard to part with him. She went home, and Thorvald set sail on the lake in a south-west gale, and it blew so hard that he and all those with him on that voyage were drowned. This news soon spread throughout the district and was thought to be a most serious matter.

The wedding feast went off well, all the same, and Gunnar was married. He and his wife set up house in the district at a farm called Bondastead, and they lived there a long time. Forthwith, in their first year they had a child, a daughter called Thordis; she was promising and became accomplished. Then in the second year they had another child, a boy called Thorkel; both children were considered promising and grew up so. These two were their eldest children; they had many others who do not come into this story. These children were given nicknames: Thorkel was called Crane, and Thordis, Bear.

IX

It is said that Droplaug felt Thorvald's death keenly, and she turned to working hard at the management of the farm. And when Bersi heard the news he left home to visit Arneidarstead, and Droplaug welcomed him most warmly as she always did.

Bersi said, 'As you know, Thorvald and I were great friends for each of us loved the other. Now I want to help you with your money matters, and so I am offering to foster your son Helgi, and I promise you that I will teach him all the human wisdom I know.'

Droplaug answered that she could not bring herself to refuse such an honourable offer for the boys, 'though now I love them more than anyone else'. Helgi was then six years old and Grim four years; both of them matured early.

Then Helgi spoke: 'I love my brother Grim so much that I won't be parted from him; we must both be at home together or both go away together.'

Bersi answered, 'It seems to me a very good thing that you are so fond of each other; I am willing to have you both whenever you like to come.' Helgi said they would be happy to stay turn and turn about with him and with their mother whom they loved very much. So they went home with Bersi, and he grew very fond of both brothers, but gave far more time to Helgi than to Grim, teaching him skills and accomplishments. They stayed there for a long time while they were young, but were longer at home when they grew older. The brothers were unlike in appearance. Grim was fair-skinned and curly-haired, and altogether good-looking. Helgi was a very big man with a broad, ruddy face and light reddish-brown hair; he was very courteous in behaviour, but his most striking feature was his ugly mouth.

X

It is related that one summer a ship put in from the sea at Reydarfiord; the owner was a woman called Groa and she was Droplaug's sister and very well off. She came to Iceland because her husband had died and she had sold her land and bought the ship; she was hoping to find her mother. Droplaug rode to the ship and asked her sister to stay with her, and she accepted that offer; the winter that Groa was there the boys Helgi and Grim were at home, and she took to them very well. These kinsfolk were all on good terms, and people noticed that the sisters were fond of each other.

When spring came, Groa asked Droplaug where she advised her to settle. Droplaug answered, 'I know some people at a good farm where their numbers are many and their means small; it seems to me that they would be willing to sell the land. The farm is called Eyvindara, it is east of Lagarfljot and that land is held to be some of the best and most attractive in the district.'

So it came about that the sisters bought that land, and Groa set up house there, and Droplaug provided her with milch cows and everything else that she needed for the farm. Groa had her ship broken up and moved the timbers over for her house building, and some of the beams are there to this day. She soon began to show great hospitality, and became very popular. She was very small but uncommonly handsome, very shrewd, ruthless, and altogether a most notable woman.

Groa had not been there long before she bred an animal that she prized above any other of her possessions. It was a stallion which she called Indoor Crow, because he was black and was stabled every winter; she soon had him gelded. Groa's livestock increased so fast at Eyvindara that you could almost believe two heads grew on every one of the creatures there. Men came from various districts to make her offers of marriage, but she turned them all down, saying that she missed her husband so much that she was determined not to marry again. Droplaug's sons paid Groa long visits, and people said they did themselves well, going round from one to another of the three best farms in the district, and being shown affection wherever they came.

It happened one day that there came a knock on the door at Bersastead, and Bersi the farmer welcomed those who had come. These were farmer Asbjorn, of Adalbol in the west, and his son Helgi. They had come on a wooing journey to ask for the hand of Bersi's daughter Thorlaug, for Helgi, Asbjorn's son. Bersi thought it over and decided that, although his daughter was a good match, no man of higher rank than Helgi was likely to seek this marriage alliance; moreover Helgi was a man blessed with many friends. So they came to an agreement, and Asbjorn made over his chieftain-ship to Helgi and put down as much money as Bersi asked for; Helgi was a most honourable man.

After that the feast was prepared, and people from far and wide about the district were invited to come. Droplaug's sons were not there, but were out at Arneidarstead. Bersi sent them word to come to the feast, but they were not much pleased about it, behaved as if they had heard nothing and did not go, but stayed at home. The feast went off very well all the same. From that time on Droplaug's sons never stayed long at Bersastead, and many people believed that Helgi Droplaugarson had wanted this woman for himself. After this Helgi Asbjarnarson settled at Oddsstead, and he and his wife got on well together.

Helgi Asbjarnarson now grew very popular and shared the chieftainship east of the lake with his kinsman Hrafnkel. The first year he and his wife were together they had a child, a girl called Ragnheid. Helgi and Thorlaug spent two years at Oddsstead, and they loved each other very much, and in the third year Thorlaug said she would like to pay a visit to Bersastead to see her father. She had weaned the little girl, and left her behind.

Thorlaug was there for a week, and then Helgi thought it was time to fetch her home, and he sent two slaves with oxen for her, and they stayed there that night. In calm weather during the night, snow fell, and in the morning they set off homewards. Now Helgi had gone up on to the rock pillar that stood up on Oddsstead headland, and he saw how they drove from the south on to the ice, and then went down into a hole where they were all drowned; that place is now called Slaves' Creek. Helgi saw the whole disaster, and took it much to heart; he went home and told the news, and many were grieved. People spoke of it all over the district, and when Bersi heard, he offered to look after the little girl Ragnheid, and fetched her home to be fostered. He thought this might help Helgi to forget sooner, but it was not so.

Helgi stayed at Oddsstead another two years and then his men urged him to marry again. He left home then, and travelled northwards over Smjorvatn Heath to Vapnafiord till he reached Hof, where a man called Bjarni Brodd-Helgason lived, a notable man and a good chieftain. He had a sister called Thordis who was a beautiful woman and most accomplished; she had a nickname and was called Thordis Todda, because she was so open-handed that when she was giving food to poor people, she gave nothing less than big portions. She was a proud and notable woman, strong, and well fitted to manage a house, though she was not much thought of at home. Helgi Asbjarnarson asked for the hand of this woman, and Bjarni gave her to him. A feast was arranged and people came to it, and when it was over Helgi rode home with his wife Thordis, who then took over the house and all the management of it. Many people thought Helgi was lucky to get her and so it turned out, for she was very wise. Soon after he was married, Helgi became known as the father of a child which had been conceived while he was a widower; it was a girl called Rannveig. The mother was the housekeeper who had been looking after his homestead. Thordis took this little girl and looked after her like one of her own family; the girl grew up there and was as pretty as the one born in wedlock, and Thordis sent the woman away, giving her plenty of money. People thought highly of the way Thordis had behaved in this matter, as also in many others.

When they had been married a year, she asked Helgi to sell that land. She felt that she could not be as hospitable as she liked because so many people came to see her. 'And I wish you would buy the farm at Mjovaness, for there I should not have such crowds at my gate.' Helgi bought the farm, and moved house. He lived there a long time until he felt forced to leave by the events that afterwards took place.

XI

A man called Thorir lived on the east side of Lagerfljot at Myness, and that farm is almost in the centre of the district. Between it and Eyvindara, where Groa lived, was a farm called Finnsstead. Thorir was an easy-going man and much liked; he had been a widower for a long time and had had various women to look after his household. Thorgrim was the name of a freedman who was nicknamed Dungbeetle; he had formerly been a fettered slave, but had worked his way to freedom. He was a member of Myness-Thorir's household and closely related to him. Thorgrim was a short man, brisk and lively, talkative, scurrilous, stupid and malicious; if he heard any man speak well of another, he flared up at once in protest, abusing people right and left.

In former times there were few 'bathrooms' in the houses. Instead, in the evening big fires were made at which people could bask; there was plenty of good firewood because every district was well wooded. The houses were so arranged that each building stood end on to another, and the rooms were narrow; the hall where people sat at mealtimes was where they slept, each in his own place, when the tables were taken up. Further within the hall were closet-beds where the most important men slept.

One evening in autumn when the people came home from haymaking, big fires were made and the farm-hands threw off their clothes to bask in front of them. Thorir was lying away from the fires on a pile of clothes, and talking with his guests.

Then Thorgrim spoke up and said, 'I often think we ought to be contented here: we've got a better master than most others, and I should say things are better here at Myness than anywhere else. And where could you find a proper match for him? A housewife who's kept up her style after her husband's death, the way he has after his wife's death?'

They all fell silent and said nothing.

Then Thorgrim answered himself, and said, 'I see I've made you lose your tongues, and that's why you've nothing to say.'

Then the farm-hand sitting on the other side of the fire, and who was the cowherd, answered. He said to Thorgrim, 'It's often your way to babble about things that are no business of yours. I know of one woman who stands out among women as Thorir does among men. Everyone would agree that she's kept up her style of living after her husband's death no less than Thorir did after his wife's. And I can tell you where she lives. Go west from here over Lagarfljot and up to Arneidarstead; the woman called Droplaug lives there, and no one could have managed better than she has since her husband's death. You wouldn't find her match anywhere in this country,' said the man, 'or further afield either,' he added.

Thorgrim answered, 'I'd do best to hold my tongue and shut up, I dare say, still I'm called Chatterbox and I'm living up to my name this evening. Droplaug was married to Thorvald Thidrandason, the most distinguished farmer in the district, and you could say that she loved him if she hadn't taken the slave Svart into her bed. Plenty of people think that Helgi Droplaugarson may be Svart's son, and not Thorvald's.'

A workman answered, 'You talk a lot about matters that other people keep to themselves, and I bet you'll be made to pay for all these lies you've been telling.'

Thorir heard what they were saying, and began to speak as he sprang up – he had a switch in his hand, and cut Thorgrim about the ears with it. He told Thorgrim to shut up and not say another word. 'Your tongue will be the death of you, I shouldn't wonder. And now all of you here in this place: if you think you owe more to me than you do to Thorgrim, I beg you to keep these words to yourselves.' Many of them promised faithfully to do as he asked, yet it turned out that not all were discreet enough to hold their tongues; so it happened as it often does, that if words leave the lips, they travel.

These words came to widow Droplaug and her sons at Arneidarstead. The boys were not at home during the day when Droplaug heard them, because every day they used to amuse themselves by going out after ptarmigan, and then bringing their catch home. They thought this the greatest sport, and did not hunt like other men, for they had no nets, but shot the birds with thonged darts. That evening they took their catch home to their mother as usual. She was always accustomed to give them a good welcome, but this time it was different; she was almost beside herself, and what little she did say was furious. She said, 'I shall be just as happy to cook for you even if you don't go after such things!'

Helgi answered, 'We don't mean to hurt you, Mother, this is just our sport; after all, people can eat the birds. Life won't be easy for us, and whether we do nothing or make a rumpus, we shall seem to be in the wrong, and I don't suppose we shall manage to please everyone.'

Droplaug answered, 'Perhaps it's because of this hunting that you seem to Thorgrim Dungbeetle to take more after the slave Svart than after Thorvald Thidrandason, or the family of the Njardvikings, or any other Icelanders I think highly of.'

Helgi answered, 'Well, Mother, I can see that you are upset in your mind, and though you think I am young, as I am, I wish you would take my advice. Take no notice of what a bad man may say; don't believe what no one else believes. Thorgrim Dungbeetle will keep on getting hold of scandal, but that won't harm you. And now, Mother, this is all the comfort I can offer you. One of two things will happen: I shall have only a short life, or the men of Fljotsdale themselves will come to say that I am not the son of the slave Svart, but of Thorvald Thidrandason, and no one is going to forget it. Please don't distress yourself about this, for I'm not going to.'

Helgi Droplaugarson was twelve years old at that time, and so well grown that he was as strong and vigorous as many a man in his prime. Grim was ten years old and most accomplished. The brothers were so fond of each other that neither would go out of the house if the other was left behind.

Droplaug turned away from this conversation and went indoors.

The boys stayed there for a long time and on into the winter. Droplaug was never as kind to them as before, but they took no notice and behaved in their usual way, and the darkest part of winter passed by. Then one night Grim felt a touch on his legs; it was bright moonlight, and he asked who was there. Helgi answered, 'Keep quiet, it's as bright as day, and I can't sleep. I want you to get up and come with me.'

'Why should we go hunting ptarmigan by night?'

Helgi answered, 'Let's go east over the lake to Eyvindara to see Aunt Groa. Mother is always gloomy, and I'm tired of it.'

Grim sprang up and dressed, and they went outside. Their everyday clothes were russet homespun tunics and breeks, with a cloak and hood for outer garment. They had thonged javelins in their hands, but neither of them had the strength to carry the sword, it was so huge. They turned down the home-meadow from Arneidarstead and on to the frozen lake.

Then Grim said, 'Why are you going on to the ice? There's no hope of any ptarmigan there. Let's turn up on to the heath.'

Helgi answered, 'I'm not going that way, because the birds are so shy if we go to the same place day after day. I'm going down over the ice to Vallaness then down from Vellir, and over Grim's river to Eyvindara.' That's what they did, because Helgi always wanted things his way.

When they came to Vallaness day was breaking, and after that, when they came out of the wood, there was no lack of birds, and they caught plenty. When they reached Eyvindara[1] it was broad daylight, and Groa welcomed them; she was delighted to see them and asked them to make a long stay. Helgi said they would, and they were there for that day. The next night before dawn Helgi was on his feet and woke his brother Grim, saying that it was good weather for hunting ptarmigan.

They got ready for a journey and went out of the farm and up to the fenced field called Uppsalir. When they got there Helgi turned down to the bog below the wood and out along the valley.

Grim asked why he was doing this. 'I'm sure the birds don't usually keep to icefields or bogs; they're more often in woods or on the moors.'

'I expect they will be there, but all the same I mean to go along the ridge above Finnsstead, and beyond Myness and out to the Snaeholt Woods. Then we shall turn up to Tokastead and so out along the fell and home to dinner at Eyvindara.'

There was frost on the ice, no wind, and the going was splendid; day was breaking as they came down the ridge above Finnsstead. They saw a stackyard which belonged to Myness-Thorir standing out into the Lagarfljot; then they saw there was a

[1] This placename is kept throughout the work, i.e. not rendered as 'Eyrind River'.

horse standing by the yard wall, and two men with it: one was making up loads and the other carrying the hay.

Helgi said, 'There are men down on the headland, and it's like enough Thorgrim Dungbeetle who is doing the loading.'

'What does it matter to you whether it's Thorgrim or another man?'

Helgi said, 'I've been told that he slandered me and my mother.'

Grim said, 'What did you tell Mother last autumn? That she shouldn't take any notice of what a bad man says. Don't go and do that yourself now.'

Helgi answered, 'Come on, I've got to see him. I want to know if there's any manhood in him but I won't do him any harm.'

XII

Now they went down over the icy slopes. The Droplaugarson brothers were easily recognized when they went out together; neither would follow the other, but they moved side by side and so people could see their tracks a long way off. Thorgrim Dungbeetle was loading in the yard, as they had seen; the cowherd was up on the wall and they were talking together. Thorgrim said, 'There are men coming down the ridges above Finnsstead. They're moving fast and I think it's likely they are the Droplaugarsons from Arneidarstead.'

The cowherd answered, 'What does it matter to us where they are going? They're fine lads and quite harmless; there's no threat to us in this journey of theirs.'

'I'm not so sure,' said Thorgrim, 'and it's my guess that they're coming to find me.'

'Why should they?' asked the cowherd. 'What can they want?'

Thorgrim answered, 'Don't you remember what we were talking about in the autumn, by the fire?'

The cowherd answered, 'Why should you worry about that? I thought it was all kept pretty quiet.'

'Don't you believe it,' said Thorgrim. 'I know that those words came to the ears of Droplaug and her sons at Arneidarstead. I've been told that they were bitter about it, and that she's been egging Helgi on to go for me. I think he's meaning to attack me now, and

I don't think I'll wait here for his revenge. I'll take the horse out of the sledge and ride home to Myness and hide there, for it's easy to see those men are coming this way.'

'I shouldn't do that,' said the cowherd; 'I should rather take the runners off the sledge and put them up on the wall, and spread a bundle of hay under our feet. The lads are only young, and they won't be able to do us much harm if we back each other up well.'

Thorgrim answered, 'I'm not going to take any risk with these devils for I think they've plenty of courage and skill. They never miss their mark whether men or birds, and they'll do for us with their darts.'

So he took the horse and leapt on its back; he had a switch in his hand and used it to beat the horse on both sides.

The cowherd said, 'It's shameful that a man like yourself should be forever cursing and abusing people, and then not dare to face those who come looking for you. I think this shows you've no spirit, and you're a coward. I'm staying here to find out what they want.'

Thorgrim lashed the horse and galloped across the headland towards the boys, then he turned the horse southwards, and waved his hand, giving a great shout, seeming to mock them. Helgi saw that and did not like it. He flung off his cloak and ran to meet Thorgrim Dungbeetle, and when he thought he was within range he hurled his dart, and it found its way in under one of Thorgrim's arms, and out under the other; Thorgrim fell dead to the ground at once. Then Helgi caught the horse and led it back to Thorgrim and set him on its back; Grim held him up, and then Helgi led the horse back to the stackyard. They greeted the cowherd quietly, and he was glad of that.

Helgi said, 'Now we have killed a man who was working with you, but the job is not yet finished, so we'd better start working along with you.'

The man answered, 'You needn't do that. I don't feel any grief; I think most people would say he's been asking for this for a long time. I shan't be working any harder because this has happened. You'd better go home the best way you can.'

Helgi said, 'Thorgrim wants to go back with you; he can't travel on his own.' He took a rope from the sledge, and bound

Thorgrim to the harness from back to front, so Dungbeetle was sitting at the back, rather bent forward.

The brothers now went back to Eyvindara, and the cowherd finished the loading at his own pace. Then he drove home, and carted the hay up to the loading port in the barn, and pitched it in; after that he fed and watered the horse while Thorgrim sat in the back of the sledge. And when the cowherd had spent the day in his own fashion he went indoors; and by then he had mucked out the cowhouse and spread the dung on the field, and all the time Thorgrim sat in the back of the sledge. Farmer Thorir was sitting at table, and it was almost noon when the cowherd told him the news. Thorir asked him why he had been so long, and he said that he had had a lot to do, 'and I didn't think it mattered much if that filthy fellow was killed'. Thorir sprang up from the table and called two men to go with him and have horses saddled.

The Droplaugarsons came back to Eyvindara and told Groa the news. She said they had done well, 'and yet it seems to me that you, my nephew, have taken early to killing for revenge'. This killing is called Helgi's first.

Groa told them not to stay long. 'You two had better ride home now to Arneidarstead,' – so they mounted Indoor Crow – 'because I think Thorir will come here to see you today. He and I will come to terms, but as for you two, goodbye now.'

They came to Arneidarstead, and their mother was in a more cheerful mood; she gave them a good welcome and asked for their news, but they said nothing at all.

'What have you been hunting since you left home?'

Helgi answered, 'I've not caught much, Mother, only one Dungbeetle.'

She answered, 'A small bird makes a small catch, but you've done well; only this particular prize of your hunting could give me such great satisfaction.' And she showed more affection to the boys than before.

Thorir now rode from home with his companions, and came to Eyvindara; he knocked on the door and called to Groa to come. She did so and greeted them. Thorir responded rather slowly and asked for the Droplaugarsons. She said they were not there, 'and yet it is as if they were here, because I will take up the case on their behalf for what happened on their journey. Fix the fine as high as you like and I will pay it. The price of a slave's killing means little to us, compared with the talk of it going the rounds. You and I have been good friends since I came to this country, and I think we should stay so; this is not such a great matter that we cannot come to terms about it.'

Thorir said that might well be. 'And because you have helped me in many ways you can settle the fine yourself.'

Groa went into the house and came out with as much money as it was usual to pay for a slave, and she gave Thorir a gold finger-ring, and commended the boys to his special charge. She said he would show friendship to her if he kept peace with the boys. Thorir said it should be as she wished, and with that he rode home.

XIII

A man called Nollar lived at the farm now called Nollarsstead which is the one nearest to Arneidarstead. He owned little property and farmed mostly with hired cattle; he had a large number of dependants. He was a very strong worker, a dark man, powerfully built; he was a scandalmonger, abusive and unpopular and disagreeable in every way. Nollar was Thorgrim Dungbeetle's brother, and thoroughly disliked. He heard what had happened in the neighbourhood and got ready to leave home; he went by night to Mjovaness to find Helgi Asbjarnarson and ask him to take up the case. Helgi was slow to reply; he said that he had not much to do with the Droplaugarsons, and that it did not matter to him if they were mixed up in such an affair. 'And it seems to me that the case belongs to Thorir; he may help you to get your legal rights, but you live near the brothers and must want to keep on good terms with them.'

Nollar answered, 'It's you I came to see, you are our chieftain, and it seems to me it's up to you to settle the difficulties of people in the neighbourhood even when our troubles aren't as bad as they are now; otherwise it's no good appealing to you.'

Helgi said, 'I'm not going to do what you ask because it seems to me that, though it is your brother who has been killed, you are both the sort of men who must expect rough treatment. So take yourself off.'

Nollar went away and thought his journey had turned out badly. He said Helgi seemed to have little authority over the Droplaugarsons, 'if they are never to be punished for their misdeeds'. Nollar took a great dislike to the brothers, but they behaved as if they knew nothing of it.

A man called Thorbjorn lived at Skeggjastead, out beyond Nollarsstead and south of Ass; he had been married but his wife was now dead and he had one daughter called Helga who was beautiful and intelligent. Thorbjorn was a wealthy man, a good farmer and well liked, and now getting on in years. Bersi the Wise was a friend of Thorbjorn's, and often accepted invitations and gifts from him. Bersi had given Helga many treasures, and it was said that he thought more of this woman than of any other, since his own wife had died. And that year people said that Helgi Droplaugarson was visiting Helga, Thorbjorn's daughter; and this was not displeasing to her as it afterwards turned out.

When the brothers had been at home two nights, Helgi caught Indoor Crow and harnessed him to the sledge; he had a cow-hide put into the sledge, asked Grim to go with him, and then they set out over the ice. They drove across the ice all the way to Skeggjastead, turned into the farm, and let the horse go in the home field, throwing down some hay for it. The brothers went into the living room and Helga welcomed them and Helgi sat down beside her. While they were talking together Helgi asked her to come over to Eyvindara and stay there for the winter, and she said she would. While they were talking this over together, another man came in, and he was wearing a dark hooded cloak. It was Nollar, and he roamed to and fro in the room keeping his hood pulled down low; then, when it was least expected, he rushed out of the house, down along the field and so down to the lake. There was a rock standing there under the banks, and he pulled off his outer clothes and threw them up on to it; then he took to his skinny legs and ran along to the end of the lake, and about midday reached Bersastead. He was wearing breeks of coarse woollen stuff and had run so fast that he was quite out of breath.

Bersi welcomed him, and asked why he had come in such a hurry.

Nollar answered, 'Because there's urgent need, as much for you as for me.'

'How so?' asked Bersi.

'Helgi, your foster-son, has come out to Skeggjastead and means to seduce Helga, Thorbjorn's daughter, away to Eyvindara and go to bed with her; and it's come to this, as the saying goes: "It's better to be betrayed than to trust no one" – because you have trusted him as you would yourself. What you have done for him can't be put into words, and now look how he repays you with what he has plenty of – wickedness and deceit.'

Bersi smiled and said, 'Why do you tell this to me rather than to anyone else?'

Nollar answered, 'Because I thought you would take it to heart and think it of the greatest importance, since everyone says you think more of her than of other women.'

Bersi replied, 'I am fond of her but not to excess, and even if Helga were given to my foster-son I should only think that a beautiful woman goes to a brave man. All the same, I think he might consider her rather beneath him in rank. As to my friendship with Helga, it's done neither of us any harm; I have given her presents because her father has given me good gifts. Now you go away, and tell your news to other people, because what you say doesn't much interest me.'

Nollar answered, 'It's true then to say that the leaders of Fljotsdale are worn-out men who let a worthless boy take their women away from them and yours the one you're so mad for that you attend to nothing else. I might as well stop telling you this, for I'm sure you'll pretend to know nothing of it even when you're disgraced. So now we see that the more familiar the terms you're on with anyone, the less you can deal with him; and the more you're insulted the less you stand up for yourself.'

Bersi answered, 'I can see you'll go the same way as your brother Thorgrim. Your talk will bring you to a bad end if you can't get decent people to help you.'

Then Bersi sprang to his feet and told his men to get ready to go with him; they caught two of his horses and saddled them. Bersi and another man rode, two went beside them on foot, and Nollar made the fifth; they went over the ice. The going was good but it was very cold, with loose, drifting snow. Helgi and Helga sat talking for a long time until it began to grow dusk. Then Helgi said she must get ready to go, 'because it's a long way to Eyvindara, and I don't want to arrive there by night'.

Helga looked about her and said, 'Wasn't Nollar here in the room for a time this morning?'

Helgi said, 'I'm sure he was, but now, all at once he's disappeared.'

Helga said, 'It wouldn't surprise me if he imagined he'd got hold of some news. I'm certainly not going with you today, for I think he has taken his story where I'd like him to be shown up as a liar.'

Helgi answered, 'Do as you like, but you can be sure that I shan't come back for you another day.'

Helga answered, 'Very well, if that's what you want, but I'm not going this time.'

Helgi went out then and sat in the sledge, and Grim mounted the horse and they went out on to the ice. Then the brothers saw men passing Nollarsstead on their way from the south over the lake, and they recognized the men.

Nollar spoke up then. 'You can see now, Bersi, whether I have been lying. There they are, driving along the ice from below Skeggjastead: Grim rides in front and Helgi and Helga are sitting in the sledge. And now, as it happens, I'm feeling very tired. I should like your leave to go home; I've a lot to do there, and I'm all on my own.'

Bersi answered, 'Go along whenever you like. I shan't often ask you to go on a journey with me, and I owe you no thanks for this one.' Nollar turned back to his farm, and Bersi and his men went on over the ice at an easy pace.

The brothers went on ahead. Both parties were following the west side of the lake until they came to the headland that juts out into Lagarfljot from the west, and is called Medalness. On the headland there stands a farm called Hreidarsstead; it is now a sheep-fold. A man called Hreidar lived there; he had settled the land, and was a good friend of Bersi and the Droplaugarsons. He was a very good farmer and a very handsome man; he had been

farming there a long time and was getting on in years. In front of
the headland there were holes in the ice, and a cowherd was
watering his cattle there; when the brothers came to the holes,
Helgi said they must water their horse, because he was hot. It was
only half-light, and they did that. Then Helgi said they should run
up into the wood, and they took out their knives and cut
brushwood. Helgi made the twigs into a bundle and tied them on
the horse's back and down under its belly with the harness strap.
He bound twigs to the tail and laid up the reins, and told the horse
to go down to Eyvindara. The twigs chafed the horse in the groin,
and he ran the faster down along the ice. Then the brothers ran up
into the wood and Helgi cut himself two staves; he stripped them
of twigs and held them in his hand.

Now Bersi and his men came to the holes in the ice, and as they
reached the south side of the headland, one of Bersi's men said, 'I
don't know how anyone can praise these men for bravery; look at
them running away from you, and you've been their best friend all
their lives. We needn't expect any great deeds from them now.'

'You are talking great nonsense,' said Bersi. 'I think, rather,
that time will show there are few to match them. Now, I want two
of you men to go to the farm at Hreidarsstead and I will ride after
the brothers with the other man, because I do not expect to need a
crowd when I meet them; there is no ill will between us. In the
meantime, you two are to wait here until I come back in the
morning.'

The men were pleased at this, and taking their clothes they
walked towards the house, laughing heartily, and saying they had
never seen such men as these: 'The more the day wears on, the
faster they run away.'

Bersi spurred his horse on over the ice. The workmen went to
the ice holes and lay down to drink, for they were hot with
running, and they laid their weapons down on the clothes they
had worn during the day. They were now in tunics and breeks.
Then Helgi said to Grim his brother, 'Let's go down and seize
them, and torment them a bit; they've been making great mock of
us.'

Grim answered, 'I'll never do that, because there's no man we
owe more to than Bersi; he's done more for us than anyone else.'

'All right,' said Helgi. 'He shall profit from the fact that he's my friend, but as for these others, that's another matter altogether. We won't put them out of action for long, but they'll find out that we can do what we like with them.' And so it was as Helgi wanted.

They ran down over the ice; each of the brothers took hold of a man, but Grim did nothing to his except to sit on him. Helgi then treated his one in this way: he crossed the man's arms over his belly and tied them together, then he forced his head back between his legs and pushed a staff under his knees so that it touched the neckbone. Then Helgi went over to Grim's man and treated him like the first. They spread the men's clothes over them and went to the farm at Hreidarsstead, knocked at the door, and called Hreidar to come out. He did so, and welcomed them and invited them to stay.

'We'll have many opportunities of accepting your offer,' said Helgi, 'but this time we're travelling late, and ought to get home tonight. All the same, I've left my mitts down by the cattle's watering-place and I really need them; it's blowing towards the sea, and I think it's going to snow. I wish you would pick them up and take them home with you this evening, when you go to water your cattle.'

Hreidar was the one man who never went to bed before a third of the night was past, and he stayed there till midday. He went indoors and the brothers made their way south to Hof, and so down below Skeggjastead. Then a storm came on and it began to snow, and worsened into a blizzard. Then Helgi turned to the farm at Nollarsstead. 'I'm going by the farms and not over the ice; I'm afraid of losing my way.' Helgi knocked on the door, and by then it was nightfall. Nollar got up out of bed and threw on his cloak; he went to the door, and as soon as he opened it, Helgi seized him by the hand and snatched him out into the storm. Grim took his other hand and they dragged him to a pile of wood and stripped his cloak off over his head. Grim stood over him by his head and Helgi pulled a switch out of the pile and thrashed Nollar till there was not a whole piece of skin from his head to his heels. Then they let him stand up and told him to clear off. 'That's what you get for your running, and there's more in store for you.' They went away and turned homewards, and when they got there it was far into the night. Droplaug welcomed them with open arms as she always did.

Bersi rode all evening till he came to Eyvindara. Indoor Crow had arrived a short time before, and a woman servant had come in out of the cowshed to tell Groa that Indoor Crow had come home strangely accoutred. Groa went out with some men and a servant with her, and they unharnessed Indoor Crow from the sledge, and fed and watered him; afterwards the man took the ropes off the sledge. Then Bersi rode into the home field and Groa welcomed him warmly. Bersi accepted her greeting and asked whether the brothers had been there. She said they had not; 'And what brings you here?'

Bersi told her the whole story as it had happened, and he stayed there that night. Groa gave Bersi and his companion a splendid meal. She commended the boys to his special charge, and asked him to show them friendship. Bersi said it should be so.

Hreidar sat reading an ancient saga[1] till dawn. Then he went out to feed his cattle, and after that he drove them to the spring. Then what Helgi had said came into his mind; he turned towards the lake and the holes in the ice, found no mitts, but saw the bundles lying there. He untied the men, and they were as stiff as logs. Hreidar went home for an ox cart, and took the men back to the farm; he looked after them well and they recovered completely. They stayed there for the night.

In the morning Bersi got ready to go home from Eyvindara; Groa gave him a gold finger-ring and a cloak fitted with straps, and said she hoped they would be fast friends. Bersi rode until he came to Hreidarsstead, where Hreidar welcomed him warmly, but his men said they had had a rough time.

Bersi laughed heartily and said, 'Young men must have their fun. No doubt they thought they had you altogether at their mercy, but for my sake they did nothing more to you than this, though they might have killed you for the outrageous way you'd behaved. Now you'd better keep quiet.'

'So we will,' they said.

They went home after that, travelling over the ice until they

[1] This is an anachronism.

came to Nollarsstead. There they saw Nollar, crouching in a corner like a dog, groaning wretchedly. He asked Bersi to take up his case, because he had endured such injuries. Bersi said that if he had suffered from the boys' quick temper, it only served him right.

'However, I will take it up though you don't deserve it.'

Nollar dragged himself indoors, and Bersi rode on till he reached Arneidarstead, and by that time it was dusk.

The Droplaugarsons were out in the home meadow, and they asked him to stay, and were glad to see their foster-father now he had come.

Bersi accepted, and was there for the night. And in the morning he had a long talk with them, chiefly about what had happened when he had ridden after them. 'And I followed you then because I wanted to warn you against letting any bad man come between us. Don't think that I will give you up as long as you leave me and my son Ormstein in peace. If you fall out with him I shall treat you both alike, but I'll back you up in any other quarrel you may have in the neighbourhood. As to the woman you have been calling on, treat her well for my sake. She and I have simply been friends, with no blame attached. I mean to keep on good terms with the father and daughter at Skeggjastead all the same, though you must make your own match as you please.'

Helgi said, 'I don't think you need worry about that from now on.'

Bersi said, 'I wish you would give that creature Nollar something for the rough way you treated him, even though he deserved it.'

Helgi said he would surely do that at his request.

Bersi got ready to go home with his men. Helgi gave Bersi two oxen, five years old, and both grey; also a chestnut stallion called Heidaraud and with him three mares. To Bersi's two workmen whom they had trussed up by the holes in the ice Helgi also gave presents: a sword to one and an axe to the other, and they parted on good terms.

Bersi went home, and the brothers stayed at home for a time. Helgi never went to see Helga again or any other woman as far as is known. And it is generally believed that Helgi was never in love with any woman, as far as is known.

XIV

It is said that one summer, a ship from abroad put in at Gautavik in Berufiord. The men on board were from Thrandheim, and they took lodgings for the winter nearby. In the spring after that winter, Thidrandi Geitisson asked his foster-father for money for a voyage: 'I want to learn about the customs of other peoples.'

Hroar answered, 'I shall take it much to heart if you want to go away from this country, because I am getting very infirm with old age, and I'm not sure you will ever come back. All the same, I will let you have as much as I can afford, but I beg you to come back as soon as you can; however, you must decide.' Hroar Tongue Priest gave Thidrandi a great deal of money; he was sad when they parted, and everyone was sorry to see Thidrandi go. He got ready for the journey and travelled south over the heath, took ship, and went abroad during the summer. They had favourable winds and made good speed; the ship came to land at Nidaross in Thrandheim.

At that time Hakon the Powerful was ruling in Norway, and he resided at Hladir. Thidrandi's good manners and breeding were obvious to everyone, and men agreed that no one in living memory had been his equal. He went to see Earl Hakon. The earl received him well, and put him to sit next to himself on the high-seat, and entertained him gladly throughout the winter. He honoured no man above Thidrandi, and they talked long together; Thidrandi's bearing was such that everyone loved him. When spring came, he asked for leave to go to Iceland. The earl asked why he only wanted to stay such a short time in Norway, 'because I am delighted to have you here as my guest. No man has ever come here whom I shall miss as much as you if you go away.'

'You have treated me very well all this time,' said Thidrandi, 'and yet I cannot bear to stay longer because I love my mother so much that I must go back as soon as I can. And I must tell you that there are still some people there who think I ought to come home sooner rather than later.'

The earl answered, 'So be it then.'

Thidrandi bought himself a ship, and had it loaded with a fine cargo of goods; the earl also gave him handsome gifts. After that

Thidrandi and his men slipped their moorings and sailed out to sea. Many people thought the truth was that Thidrandi had found it difficult to put up with the earl's temper, and that was why he did not want to stay longer.

Thidrandi got good winds that summer, and sailed his ship into Skalavik in Vapnafiord; he unloaded the ship, moved his cargo home, and after that fenced the ship and had it laid up. He went home to Krossavik, where he was given a most joyful welcome; there was also a most affectionate meeting between himself and Hroar. He had stayed there only a few nights when Hroar announced that he wanted Thidrandi to go east with him, to his own estate and domain, 'because I love Thidrandi so much that I cannot bear to be parted from him; every hour seems long when he is not near me'.

Thidrandi said he would go as soon as Hroar liked; 'I'll enjoy your company while I have the chance.'

Thidrandi got ready to travel and rode east with Hroar to Hof in Hroar's Tongue, and when they came to Vapnafiord his kinsmen there were delighted. All his kinsmen rejoiced that he had come back with so much honour.

Ketil Thrym sent word to his nephew Thidrandi, inviting him to a feast at Njardvik, and said he should not come for nothing, 'for he is the only one of my kinsmen whom I should relish being on good terms with'.

Thidrandi promised to go late in the summer when haymaking was finished; he said he would not have the leisure to come before that, as he had already promised to visit other people. Ketil said that Thidrandi was quite right.

XV

There was a man called Asbjorn, who was a southerner, and newly arrived in the Fljotsdale district. He was a native of Floi in the south, and he had travelled east from there to Rangarvellir, then east again to Sida, and had not stopped until he reached Fljotsdale in the east, where he took board lodgings. Asbjorn was a tall man with dark hair, he had an ugly face and was rather disagreeable, yet many men were tempted to seek him out because he was so great as a wall builder that he had no equal; he had a nickname, and was called Wall-hammer. Asbjorn had been five years in Fljotsdale at this time, and had built walls round home meadows and also boundary walls; the proof that he was such a master builder may be seen in walls of his building that still stand in the East Fiords.

There was a man called Thorbjorn, known as Korek, who lived in the farm called Koreksstead, east of Lagarfljot, by the eastern fells in Utmannasveit. Thorbjorn had a wife who was related to the Njardvikings, and he had two sons, the elder called Gunnstein and the younger Thorkel: Thorkel was then eighteen and Gunnstein twenty-two. They were both big men, strong and very courageous, but Thorbjorn was now very old. Asbjorn Wall-hammer had been with him two years and had made some money. In his third year he set up a farm for himself because his wife was pregnant; he had also other children, and beyond the brook he rented some land which was then called Sheepbrook but is now known as Hlaupandastead, and he was there for a year. He had not much livestock, and found himself in difficulties; in the summer he left his home to go and see Ketil out in Njardvik, and asked if he would take him on as a workman. Ketil asked why he wanted to give up farming, and he replied that he found it all touch and go, living in such sore straits.

Ketil said, 'You seem to me to have too big a family.'

Asbjorn said he was only seeking a place for himself, and would make other arrangements for his family.

Ketil asked what arrangements he was going to make for his family, and he said that he intended to run away from them, 'and come here to you, because if I'm under your protection no one will molest me much. I'll let the woman look after the children.'

Ketil said, 'I have often thought of taking you on, and now I'll offer you terms. You shall build a wall down from the fell, under the cliffs and down to the sea, for two years' board and lodging.'

Asbjorn said he would easily carry out that work. 'We'll strike the bargain this way, and your share shall be to keep my past life from catching up on me.' Ketil agreed to this.

Afterwards Asbjorn went up over the heath, fetched his bedding, and ran away from his family, so that the place is now called Hlaupandastead.[1] The people at Koreksstead took over his dependants but lost his land rents and got into all manner of difficulties. Asbjorn began to build the wall in Njardvik down from the fell. He did a good deal of work during the summer, but his disposition did not change, and no one liked him except Ketil.

XVI

Thidrandi made ready to leave home in the seventh week of summer.[2] Taking six men with him he rode out along Lagarfljot and down along Hroar's Tongue, crossing the river at Bakkaford, then up-country, reaching Thorbjorn at Koreksstead in the evening. Thorbjorn and his sons went out to meet Thidrandi and his party, and in friendly fashion invited him to stay there as long as he liked. He was there for the night, and they entertained him splendidly. The brothers asked him if he would be willing to go out to Njardvik and ask Ketil to release Asbjorn and pay his summer wages, or else to take on his family as well as himself.

Thidrandi said he would be willing to talk it over, but, 'on the other hand I don't wish to do more than that, because Ketil is my kinsman'.

They said that seemed to them reasonable enough.

After that night was over they got ready, twenty men in all. They rode to Oss, and down the heath by a pass called Gongkuskard and on to the bay.

It was mid-evening when they reached the bay, and there were few people at home; they were still haymaking, for much of the land there was under grass. All the men were out at work, except for Ketil, who was at home with some women. He was sitting in the main room, and they say that just then the shivering he was subject to came over him, so that he shook from his feet up and every tooth in his head rattled. He shuddered as if cold water were being poured between his skin and his flesh. Then he called out to a woman to make a fire to warm himself by; he flung down a sheepskin, and baked and rubbed himself on it by the fire.

---

[1] Runningstead.
[2] In the old reckoning this would be some time late in May.

Thidrandi and his men rode down along the bay, and when they had almost reached the farm they saw a man up on the hillside, building a wall. He was wearing a grey tunic with its skirt hitched up to his shoulders, and loops hanging down at the sides. He wore a coarse white overall, and had pulled the hood over his head; they realized that this was Asbjorn Wall-hammer. He said nothing to them in greeting, so they rode down along the wall without speaking to him.

Then Gunnstein Koreksson rode down to Thidrandi and said, 'That man is behaving in a unpleasant sort of manner; won't you give me leave to draw the pin from my spearhead and let fly at him, just to see how he takes it?'

'Don't do that,' said Thidrandi. 'There's an old saying that "wrong begets wrong", and I don't want you to have anything to do with him.'

Then Gunnstein turned away, and went to the rear of the company, and off the pathway. He pulled the pin out of his spearhead and shot at Asbjorn, laughing loudly. When Asbjorn saw the spear coming at him, he leapt up and it went into the skirt of his tunic and through the loops, and out into the new wall, so that he fell off it. He jumped up at once, throwing the spear down; then he leapt up on to the wall and down the other side, and raced off home to the farm.

When he reached the home meadow he ran into the room where Ketil was roasting himself by the fire, and threw himself on to the seat opposite the fire.

Ketil asked him what was the matter.

'It's hard to know what to do for the best,' he answered. 'When I came here in the spring, I never thought I should be knocked about and beaten almost to death; but here come these Korekssons, and Gunnstein shot his spear in under my one arm and out under the other. I'd thought I was coming to live with a chieftain, but now I can see you're good for nothing; you never avenge our injuries, however shaming they are.'

Asbjorn had raised his voice and was gasping for breath.

Ketil sprang up in a great rage. He snatched up a woollen tunic and pulled it on – before that he was wearing only footless trews, strapped under his feet, as no one wore linen breeks at that time.

Without a word Ketil strode through the kitchen, with sparks
from the fire flying all round him, till he came to the closet-bed
where he usually slept. He reached for a helmet and put it on his
head, took his sword in his hand and set a shield before him; then
he turned to go out, drawing his sword and throwing down the
scabbard.

Just as Ketil reached the home meadow, Thidrandi and his men
rode into it. Ketil turned on Thidrandi at once and struck at him
with his sword. The blow came so close that Thidrandi had no
time to throw his shield before him. He jerked himself out of the
saddle – at that time men rode on high decorated saddles[1] – and
landed on his feet, but Ketil's stroke followed through and cut the
saddle in two, lengthways through the bows, and went through
the horse under it. Ketil cut at Thidrandi a second time; he got his
shield before him then, but Ketil clove it alongside the grip, so that
the sword struck the ground.

Some of the women in the farmhouse ran up to where the men
were at work, and others ran down to another farm on the bay
called Virkihus, because some men were still at home there; they
came along too, and there were twenty men in all.

Thidrandi told his men not to attack Ketil, 'and if anyone
disobeys me I shall go for him myself, even if he is one of my own
men'.

After that, Thidrandi offered his kinsman Ketil a full reconcilia-
tion. 'I had not expected this sort of welcome, but if you want to
talk over what has been happening since we came, I will pay any
compensation you think honourable. Now, if you give no weight
to my words, let me remind you that my mother is your sister, and
that you are taking a big risk if you go on in this way.'

Ketil kept silent. Thidrandi asked him again to be reasonable
but Ketil launched a furious attack on him as if no one else were
there.

'It seems a pity', said Thidrandi, 'that a man should go on like
this when there's no need. But no one is to attack Ketil; he'll soon
calm down, and I'm not asking any of you to kill his men.' So they

[1] These saddles had high bows back and front, and are mentioned in documents
from the thirteenth century.

pulled out as they could, and then turned away southwards over the home meadow.

It was now late in the evening and the sun was low; the horses were straying here and there because every man had dismounted as he arrived. They all bore south along the wall until they came to the brook that flows outside the fence below the house. Then Thidrandi thrust the point of his sword into the bank and leapt backwards over the brook; his shield had been hacked to pieces, so that not an inch was left except round the grip. At this moment Ketil struck at Thidrandi and hit his right shoulder so that the shoulder-blade and part of the lung were laid bare. Thidrandi sprang down, back over the brook, changed his sword into his left hand and thrust at Ketil; the sword went right through him, and he fell dead to the ground, but Thidrandi went southwards over the brook, walked to the knoll below the path which is now called Thidrandi's Knoll, and there he sat down. Thorkel and Gunnstein, the Korekssons, were the only other men left on their feet; all the rest of Thidrandi's men had fallen. The Korekssons sat one on each side of Thidrandi, and they were quite worn out.

Ketil's men crowded round him, and covered his dead body; after that they went home weary with fighting, and many were wounded.

Now Thidrandi began to speak. 'Gunnstein,' he said quietly, 'what do you mean to do? Is it any good to hand out blame for what has happened? If only you hadn't taken the law into your own hands – but it's no use blaming you now. And have you seen that fellow Asbjorn this evening?'

'I've had other things to do than bother about that devil,' answered Gunnstein.

'Well,' said Thidrandi, 'I've not been too busy to keep an eye on what he's been up to. This evening when Ketil ran out and men went for him, Asbjorn came out too and was shading his eyes with his hand to see how things were going between us. Now he's gallantly retreated; I think he's in the field beyond the brook, and it's my guess that he's stripping a dead body.'

Then Gunnstein saw where Asbjorn was, and jumped over the brook. He had his sword in his hand, and struck Asbjorn on the back, and cut him asunder through the middle. After that he went back to where he had been sitting.

A woman went out in the evening – she was a woman servant.

XVII

There was a man called Gunmar who was boarding with Ketil; he was a Norwegian, and had come out to Iceland in the summer. He was from a Halogaland family and was a big, warlike man, young and very accomplished; he was sitting in a store-house behind the main building where his goods were kept. He had not been at the fighting, or known that it had happened. A woman ran to his store-house; she was the servant who worked for him. Gunnar was sitting in the doorway feathering arrows when she burst out, 'It's true what they say that no one can see a man who's not there at all. When Ketil asked you here in the autumn he can't have imagined he would get no help from you when he needed it. And you're all the more of a foul wretch lying indoors like a bitch with whelps while the man of the house lies dead in the field, and many of his men with him. There are raiders here, and they've killed Ketil.'

Gunnar jumped up at this news, caught up his bow, and put the arrow he had just made to the string. He ran outside, asking, 'Have they got away, the men who did this evil deed?'

She said, 'No, indeed.'

'Then where are they?' he asked.

'The ones who are still alive are in the field, south of the brook.'

'Where is Thidrandi?' asked Gunnar. 'I want to see him.'

'I think,' she said, 'that he is sitting on the Bird Knoll between the Koreksson brothers.'

Gunnar bent his bow, and just as the string twanged in the farmstead Thidrandi fell backwards; the arrow pierced his chest and went out between his shoulders. Gunnar asked who the man was.

She answered, 'That was Thidrandi Geitisson.'

'Most wretched woman, there was no man better liked or more accomplished. He is the very last man I would have chosen to kill.'

Thorkel Koreksson asked his brother Gunnstein if he were much wounded. Gunnstein said he had a slight wound, 'but what about you, Thorkel?'

'I don't think it's a bad wound,' said Thorkel. 'Now we've no need to wait for Thidrandi, and we'd better not go to the farm. I don't believe we shall get our horses, and I don't think it will be very easy walking.'

They turned a shield over Thidrandi, there on the knoll, and afterwards walked away straight up the slope to the path. They walked slowly because it was a very dark night. They went on until they reached the slopes below the mountain pass where there was a grassy hollow south of the path, called Kidjahvamm. A river flows down from the pass and into the hollow where there was a big waterfall, and under the waterfall a big cave. In the autumn men often shelter there when they go up into the mountain to round up sheep.

Thorkel said, 'Let's go into the cave; I'm worn out. I can't go any further.' They went into the cave and there was a pile of stones in front of it. Gunnstein threw himself down there; he was very hot and took off his clothes. Thorkel loosened his belt, then he stripped off his clothes and his entrails fell out; he sat down, and his life came to an end. He had come all the way up from Njardvik in this state. Now Gunnstein was alone after his brother died, and he was badly wounded. He decided that his best course was to go away from that place, and he stood up, but when he tried to walk he was so stiff that he could not put one foot in front of the other. He sat down again, and there he had to stay, though he did not like it.

Thorbjorn Korek had bad dreams that night, and when he woke up he hastened to get dressed. He roused the shepherd and said he must go on an errand: 'I want you to take two horses, and I want you to ride out to Oss, and over to the cave in Gongkuskard which you use for night quarters in the autumn when you go to round up the sheep. Be on the look-out there, and if you find anything out of the way, I shall be glad to know of it.' The shepherd rode to Oss and over to Gongkuskard and looked about for travellers, and when he came to Kidjahvamm, he dismounted. By that time day was breaking and he went in under the waterfall and into the cave. He called out to ask if there was anything there that could answer him, and Gunnstein gave his name. The shepherd asked him for news, and Gunnstein told him what had happened. The shepherd asked if he should take him away, and Gunnstein said that was the only thing to be done. He wanted to go out at once but he could not walk unless he leant on the shepherd's shoulder and went on one leg. The shepherd got him into the saddle, and put his clothes round him and held him up as best he could. They rode over the heath and came home about noon. Thorbjorn had got a bath ready; he cleaned Gunnstein's wound and gave him what relief he could.

XVIII

This news soon spread abroad, and many thought it serious as indeed it was. It struck nearest to Hroar Tongue Priest, who took to his bed in sorrow and died of grief. After the fight Thorkel the Very Wise came home, because he had been down the fiord after dried fish; he reached home the day after the night battle, and heard the news that his father and Thidrandi had been killed. He raised a burial mound over Thidrandi his kinsman, and it stands on the bank below the farm; and he buried the men who had fallen in another mound. He drove the Norwegian away with insults and abuse, saying he had done a most shameful thing and one for which no compensation could be fixed: he had killed the man who would have given the greatest joy to many. Gunnar disappeared and nothing was heard of him.

Many people were grieved at the news when they heard it, and thought these were great events. Thidrandi's brother, Thorkel Geitisson, Bjarni Helgason of Hof in Vapnafiord, because he was a near kinsman of Thidrandi's, Bjarni's sister Thordis Todda who was married to Helgi Asbjarnarson, also the two brothers Grim and Helgi the sons of Thorvald Thidrandason – these were all wanting to avenge Thidrandi and looking for Gunnar the Norwegian, but there was no word of him. Most people thought that he must have run away to find the other Norwegians who had laid up their ship, and camped near to it in a bay between Njardvik and Borgarfiord, on the other side of Snotruness. There were seventeen Norwegians there, and this made people think he would have gone to them.

Now winter passed by and the days grew longer; then Thorkel

Geitisson set out from Krossavik in the north with nine men, to go east over the heath. He rode up the west side of the lake till he came to Arneidarstead; Droplaug and her sons greeted him well and he stayed the night there. Then he asked those brothers if they would go down to Njardvik with him to see Thorkel Very Wise, and thence southwards to the fiord. 'I want to get hold of the man Gunnar who is now called Thidrandi-killer. He has caused us much grief; we all need to get rid of him.'

The brothers now got ready to go with Thorkel, and they went down the valley, recruiting men here and there until they were eighteen in all. Now they travelled on until they came to Thorbjorn at Koreksstead in the evening. They were invited to stay and were there for the night. They questioned Gunnstein in great detail about what had been done at Njardvik in the autumn, and he told them clearly enough, but was unwilling to talk about it. And when a third of the night had passed Helgi Droplaugarson got up; it was bright moonlight, and there was good going both on the heath and in the valley, and he woke his companions. Then he went to Gunnstein and spoke to him: 'You will be wanting to come out to Njardvik with us, cousin.' Gunnstein answered, 'I'll come if you want me to.'

After that they got ready to travel and went out below Sandbrekka, and so out to Oss and up onto the heath by Gongkuskard, until they came to where there was a slope and a grassy hollow beside the path called Deep Hollow. In the summer the path runs to the south of the hollow, but in the winter, when snow lies there, men go down along the hollow. Helgi turned off the path and sat down; he got all the others to sit down and ranged them in a row with a gap in the middle, like the one in a yard wall.

Thorkel Geitisson said, 'What are you doing this for, kinsman?' Helgi answered, 'I thought I heard men's voices a little while ago, up on the pass. Like this, we can seize those men whoever they are.'

When they had sat down again, five men came swinging at them on iron-spiked mountain staves, all wearing steel helmets and girt with swords. They knew these men, for they were Thorkel Very Wise from down at Njardvik and his men. Helgi and the others jumped up and he told them to seize hold of these men, and they did so. Then Helgi went to Thorkel and greeted him, and asked where he was going. Thorkel said he was going into the country to collect debts.

'Why do you tell me such an unlikely story?' asked Helgi. 'It's not the time of year to go out on money matters. I can see that this is not your business, and I think I know what is, and where you are going, and that is to Mjovaness. You are going to hand Gunnar Thidrandi-killer over to Helgi Asbjarnarson, thinking he is the most likely man to protect Gunnar from me. You must know that he and I are on bad terms.'

Thorkel answered, 'Why should you think I would choose to protect the man who has brought such great shame on us? And you will have heard that I sent him away the very day I got home.'

'I don't care what you say about this,' said Helgi. 'You'd better make your choice at once: either I kill you here in Deep Hollow, or you hand over that man.'

Thorkel said he did not know where the man had gone.

Then Helgi stripped Thorkel and all his companions of their weapons and clothes; he made them lie down, and set an equal number of his own men to work on them. Helgi said, 'If you won't behave as if you were my kinsman you'll be no loss to us and I'm not going to spare you now.'

Then Thorkel saw the dilemma he was in, and he said, 'You are a hard man to deal with. I'm like most people: I want to stay alive if I can, so I'll tell you the truth now. I have been looking after the Norwegian; I had him all last winter, since the fight. I was shamming when I said he'd gone away. Up on the heath above Njardvik farm there's a ledge running south from the pass over Skalaness. Opposite the farm there's been a landslide from the ridge on to the ledge, and those boulders are all overgrown with moss and lichen.

'When I drove him away in the autumn I put up a tent among the boulders; it is iron grey, the same colour as the stones, and I put his leather sleeping bag in it, and settled him in as well as I could. He's been there ever since.'

Then Helgi answered, 'Now you've done the right thing, telling me the truth; all the same I knew beforehand that you were keeping him. I'll do you no harm now, but you can't go free as things are.'

Then Helgi spoke to Thorkel Geitisson and asked, 'Would you rather go down over the heath and fetch the Norwegian, or will you stay here until noon, guarding your namesake?'

Thorkel Geitisson answered, 'I would rather stay here with my namesake, and guard him. We Vapnfiordings are no great champions, and here I shan't have much to do. I think looking for Gunnar will be a test of luck, and I've more faith in the strength of your luck than mine.'

'I gave you the choice,' said Helgi, 'because I thought you had better choose for yourself; but we can't tell how things are going to turn out. Now I'm going to divide our company into two. We two brothers with eight men will go down over the heath to find out if we're on the right track, and you and your company are to go up to Arneidarstead in the evening, and wait there for me until I come in the morning; if we don't find the Norwegian I'll come at midday. If Thorkel Very Wise has lied he will have to be killed, but if he is speaking the truth he can't be blamed even if Gunnar has got away. If I don't come by midday you are to let Thorkel go wherever he likes, because by then I shall have found the track of the Norwegian whether I have my hands on him or not.'

And now they parted; Helgi and his men went down over the heath and Thorkel Geitisson sat down beside his namesake. When Helgi came to the pass, day was breaking; over the sea hung heavy clouds which quickly spread over the sky, and it began to snow with a north-east wind. They pushed on down the slopes and then they saw where the ledge ran along the mountainside.

Then Grim Droplaugarson said, 'Let's not do the work twice; let's turn out along the ledge from here.' They had not gone far when they saw the fall of rocks and the tent. It was then half-light, and the snow drifted more and the wind grew stronger, and it was very cold. About this time the Norwegian woke up in his tent and had to go outside to relieve himself; he got up in tunic and linen breeks, and pulled on his shoes, but did not button them.[1] He had nothing on his head and nothing in his hand, and when he was fastening his breeks he heard men's voices to the south along the ledge; and they were near the tent. He saw that it was useless to go back into the tent, his enemies had got so near, so he turned out

---

[1] These buttoned shoes would be foreign ones.

along the ledge as far as he could go. They saw him then, and thought they had him within their grasp for they did not believe he could get far. Each man urged the others to go after him. Gunnar ran as fast as his legs would carry him, so that he lost his shoes. Now the distance between them increased, as Gunnar was quite fresh; he ran down beside the fishing shed and out of the hollow, then he stopped and tied his linen breeks to his ankles. The others had come down past the fishing shed on to level ground, and they drew up in a row down to the sea. Grim was their swiftest runner; he sprang out from the band and ran at Gunnar, meaning to wound him. Gúnnar saw this, threw himself into the sea, and at once began to swim. Grim saw that he could not kill him in hand-to-hand fighting so he flung a spear after him and it hit Gunnar's left hand; he took hold of it and pulled it out and struck out across the bay. The wind was keen and the waves were rough.

Helgi spoke and said, 'Where shall we find another man of such courage, and who is going to go after him?' No one offered to take this risk.

'I'm not surprised at this,' said Helgi, 'for either he or one of us would perish and no one is to make the attempt, for to land where Gunnar was already ashore would be a most chancy business, and in any case we don't know how well he can swim. I think we had better go on to the boat-house and see if we can find a boat to row after him, though it will slow us down rather. And we still have to watch where he's heading for.'

Helgi and his companions did as he said, and Gunnar swam across the bay and came ashore south of the landslide where it is now called Gunnarsdale. Men who have compared the two, say that the distance Gunnar swam across Njardvik was equal to that from Naustadale over to Vindgja. Gunnar then ran up on to Snotruness; his own crewmates were living in a hut on the far side of the headland, and he went to find them there.

The Droplaugarsons and the others rowed across the bay and came to land soon after Gunnar. They beached the boat, and started after Gunnar when they saw where he was going, rushing pell-mell after him. Gunnar ran into the hut where people were sitting at breakfast and asked them to help him. 'Help me to make a stand, then we'll get the better of the men who are after me.'

They said they were not going to run themselves into danger because of his misfortunes. He called the bay Nanny-goat Bay after his comrades and that has been its name ever since. And when he saw that he would get no help from them he turned away, and up on to Snotruness; he made south to Borgarfiord, no better equipped than before. The Droplaugarsons saw that Gunnar was running away from the bay, so they did not go that way; they ran high above the huts. Gunnar's feet now began to be very numb; he had run barefoot over hard frozen ground, and it was very cold: his linen clothes froze on him. On his run he had exerted himself to the limit of his strength and that had helped to keep him warm. They had been catching up with him until he came up on to the ridge that slopes away to the south.

XIX

South under the ridge stands a farm called Bakki, and they thought that was the nearest. A man called Sveinung lived there, and he was a big, strong man and well off; he was married and had one son who was then nine years old. He and his son were the only men on the farm, but there were several women there. Sveinung kept much to himself and people thought there was something uncanny about him. Yet he could be all right when he felt like it, though he usually kept out of people's way.

The day Gunnar passed that way Sveinung had gone to fetch peat. He was loading the sledge and had filled the baskets but not the gaps between them, when Gunnar came running along. He ran up to Sveinung crying out, 'Save me!'

'What from?' asked Sveinung.

'My enemies are after me, and if they catch me they'll kill me,' said Gunnar. Sveinung asked who he was.

'My name is Gunnar, and I am called Thidrandi-killer,' he answered.

Sveinung asked, 'Who are chasing you?'

'I'm not sure,' replied Gunnar, 'but I think it's the Droplaugarsons.'

'That's all right then,' said Sveinung, 'and I won't ask any more about your offence. All the same, I'm glad to know that you're getting some punishment for your crime – killing the man everyone thought so much of.'

Gunnar answered, 'I can't deny it's a bad thing to have done. There's no need to remind me of it, but it's up to every man to save himself while he can.'

Sveinung said, 'You can lie down between the baskets if you like, but that won't be much use against the sort of champions who are after you.'

Sveinung took off his cloak and wrapped it round Gunnar who then lay down on the sledge between the baskets; then Sveinung grasped the reins of the horse and never stopped till he came home to Bakki. And when Gunnar lay down on the sledge the ridge came between him and his pursuers; the Droplaugarsons were west of the ridge and the peat was to the east, and so they did not see him.

Sveinung drove the sledge across the doorway, and the young lad was standing there; he was wearing a white tunic and breeks made of ordinary woollen stuff. Sveinung said to the boy, 'Take your staff and run south up the fell and get our sheep down into shelter; it looks like bad weather coming.'

The boy said, 'I'll just get my hood and my mitts from indoors.'

'When I was young,' said Sveinung, 'we needed neither hood nor mitts.'

So the boy ran off as fast as he could, for he was afraid of his father. Sveinung unhitched the horse from the sledge and led it to the spring, and afterwards into the stable. Then he went back to the house, untied the ropes from the sledge and tipped it up against the wall.

Just then the Droplaugarsons came into the home meadow. Sveinung gave them a friendly greeting and they replied in the same way. Sveinung asked what they had come for – Helgi asked if he had seen a man running past him a little while before 'when you were carting peat'.

'I saw no one but myself. You are welcome to such hospitality as you may like to take.'

Helgi said they needed nothing; 'there's a great part of the day yet to come. What I want to know is about the man who was running past the peat cuttings earlier on. I can't see how you could have missed him.'

Sveinung answered, 'I'm not sure that I didn't see a man running down from the peat cuttings a short time ago; he was in light-coloured clothes, and now that same man is running south up the fell.'

He raised his hand and pointed, and they saw where a man was running. Helgi now urged his companions to go after him, and they did so.

When the boy had run off, Sveinung had unloaded the sledge in the porch; Gunnar was lying there under the peat with the baskets on top of him when the Droplaugarsons arrived. As soon as they were away Sveinung cleared off the peat. He drew his knife from the sheath and cut Gunnar's clothes off him, took him into the barn, and got him up into the middle of the haystack. After that Sveinung went indoors and stacked the peat.

The Droplaugarsons went south over the Brunnlaek Springs in the southern part of the meadows. Then Helgi stopped short, stood still, and said, 'That man running up the fell is going swiftly for a man who's not long come from a swim; I should have thought he'd be pretty well tired out with running barefoot over frozen ground all day. Anyway, isn't that man calling up sheep?'

'What of that?' answered Gunnstein Thorbjarnarson. 'He'll be doing it as a blind.'

Helgi answered, 'He doesn't look to me the sort of man I'd expected Gunnar to be. Hasn't Sveinung played a trick on us by sending his son off to call in sheep, while he hid Gunnar and let him escape? We won't chase that man any more, we'll turn back and deal with farmer Sveinung.' So they went back to the farm.

Sveinung was in the porch stacking peat, and said, 'Why have you come back so soon?'

'Because we think you are hiding the man,' replied Helgi. 'He's not up the fell as you said; that's your son.'

'I thought he was indoors in the living room,' answered Sveinung; 'However, I don't see how I can be hiding Gunnar now.'

Helgi said, 'You must have put him between the baskets and tipped him out with the peat; we ought to have found him. Now we're going to make a search.'

'You have the power to do this,' said Sveinung, 'because of your numbers; but this is the first time I've had my house ransacked as if I were a thief.' So they went in and searched the house but did not find him.

Then Helgi said, 'We'll go to the cowshed and the barn, both of them.'

'You'll see the Norwegian in there all right,' answered Sveinung; 'that cow makes plenty of muck!'

'I've no time for your jokes,' said Helgi.

Sveinung went to his bed and took down a big one-edged sword nine ells[1] long, and fastened it on. Then he went to the cowshed and opened it up, and he turned to Helgi and said:

'Helgi, you're a great lawyer, and you must know what the law is, to wit that no more men should enter a house than there are men inside it. Now I am alone. I wish only one of you to go in, because there are no more hiding-places in my cow-stalls and goat-pens than you will see straight away. I don't want men racketing about and harming my animals with their weapons. There are gangways all round the hay in the barn; it's dark in there, because in the autumn I had it filled with hay from the outfields, and I blocked up all the windows with muck and that's frozen hard. Let your men break in the windows, and you, Helgi, go in with me and search.'

Helgi said, 'I'll do as you advise.'

Sveinung went into the cowshed and Helgi with him, while Grim and his men broke in the windows, which was slow work for it was all frozen hard. Helgi searched the stalls and pens in the cowshed. After that they went to the barn.

Then Sveinung said, 'Now you stand in the doorway and I'll go into the barn and walk all round the hay. Then I'll go up on to the stack and turn over the wet hay. You can't go up there till I've shifted it; you being something of a dandy I wouldn't want you to get your clothes dirty.'

Sveinung then climbed up on to the hay, and he made the Norwegian lie down in the very middle of the stack and covered him with big slabs of hard old hay, and then threw all the loose hay off the middle of the stack, letting the slabs lie. And when he was turning the third slab, they broke through the windows and

---

[1] This kind of exaggeration is typical of 'lying sagas'.

let light into the barn, so they could see there were no hidden corners.

Then Sveinung stood up on the stack and said, 'Now you have seen every hiding-place here, so now you must search the loose hay, and turn it all over on to the slabs. Either he's in the hay, or he's not here. You can go and break up the slabs if you want to, but I shall stand by.'

Helgi did not like that. 'I've no mind to break all that up and I don't think we need go on searching here,' he said.

After that they went away, with no farewell to Sveinung. They went the same way as before, and when they reached the south side of the farm they met the boy driving the sheep towards them.

As soon as the Droplaugarsons had gone, Sveinung took the Norwegian away but left the slabs of hay lying where they were. He took Gunnar down to his boat-house by the sea. In front of it was a ship[1] upside-down, in which, in the autumn, Sveinung had brought cargo from south down the fiord. The prow and stern were buried in the ground, and snow had drifted up to the gunwales. Sveinung kept sheep inside it during hard weather; he now took a spade, dug in under the gunwale and made Gunnar crawl in under the ship, and he shovelled snow and sheep muck up to it. Just then the boy came with the sheep, so they drove them in and closed the shed. The sheep trampled the snow so that new marks were hidden, and Sveinung stayed there stamping about, but the boy went home.

The Droplaugarsons left the homestead, striking south. Then Helgi stopped short and said, 'I think it's like the saying, I'm wise after the event. It seems to me we've still not made a proper search here.'

'Where do you think he could have been?' asked Grim.

'Sveinung tipped three slabs out of the hay,' said Helgi, 'and I thought the first was the heaviest; he said I could go right up to it, but it was dark then.'

Grim said, 'Why didn't you see this till now?'

'Because it didn't seem as likely to me then as it does now,' answered Helgi. 'Now we must turn back again.' The fact is that many people think Helgi lacked courage when just the two of

[1] Later the ship is said to be inside the boat-shed.

them were in the barn, and that he may have seen Gunnar then, but thought it unwise to do anything.

Grim said, 'Shall we go back to the cowshed then?'

'No,' said Helgi, 'I don't think we need do that.' So they went down over the meadow.

By that time Sveinung had come up off the foreshore by way of the cliffs. When they met, Sveinung said, 'On the wrong track again, Helgi?'

He answered, 'It may look like that to you.'

'Where will you look now?' said Sveinung.

'I don't think we've searched your quarters well enough,' said Helgi.

Sveinung smiled, and said, 'Where can he have been?'

Helgi said, 'It's my guess that he was in the first slab of hay you turned over; it seemed the heaviest.'

'Then I'd better go and get my claws on him,' said Sveinung.

'You've played us a trick,' answered Helgi, 'and got him away somewhere else.'

'Well, where will you look this time?' said Sveinung.

Helgi answered, 'I'm going to search for him now, in your boat-house.'

Sveinung said, 'It's far more likely the ewe-lambs have caught him; they have all their wits about them. But I've shut a lot of sheep up in there, and if you break open the shed I shall make you responsible for what happens, because the sheep will be down on to the shore straight away, and there's an offshore wind blowing. Here in Borgarfiord a flood-tide can carry sheep away; it has been known to happen. Now if you let the sheep out and don't drive them in again, I shall claim for damage both by storm and high tide. I have a ship in there which I turned over last autumn, and it is the only hiding-place there. You'll have to shift it to find anything, so now if anything happens to it you're responsible, as well as for the other matters.'

'I don't care,' answered Helgi. 'I don't know what I shall have to answer for. We're going to search all over again.'

Helgi went down the narrow cliff path; Sveinung sat down at the top and stared out to sea.

They went to the shed and drove out the sheep. Then Helgi said,

'It's just as Sveinung said; there's nowhere to hide except under the ship. You must hack down everything round it, and then we'll move it aside.'

Then Grim spoke. 'There's no need to do that, brother,' he said. 'Let's rather thrust our spears in under the gunwhale, then we shall find out if there's anything there. We can't open up the ship without breaking parts of it, and it would be a shame to smash such a valuable thing.'

So that's what they did, thrusting their spears in all round under the ship. Gunnar was aware of what they were doing, and he gripped the ribs of the ship, and braced his feet against the timbers, and coiled up above while they laid on down below. He got a great wound from one man's spear, which pierced his thigh near the buttock, and it was a serious injury. Gunnar did not flinch at this wounding, and the man holding the spear only thought he had pushed it into the snow. When they had searched to their satisfaction they made off, leaving the boat-house without driving the sheep in again. They went up the cliff path, and Sveinung was sitting there at the top. He said not a word to them and he was in a rage, changing colour, sometimes as pale as bast and sometimes as dark as earth while most of his hair stood on end. They thought they could see that he was in an angry mood and kept out of his way, for they believed he would have made a troll-change before them if they had found the Norwegian.

After that the Droplaugarsons went away, and Sveinung went to the Norwegian and took him home that evening into his own room and bound up his wound. Later on he took Gunnar into an underground room that he had, away from the farmstead.

The Droplaugarsons held south along the mountainside and kept on south to Dysjarmyr, reaching it after sunset, and they knocked on the door. A man called Gunnstein lived there; he was the Borgarfiord Godi, and had authority there. He was a full brother of Sveinung, and a very big, strong man; a good farmer, but a very hard man to deal with. It was common talk among men that Gunnstein was of the same nature as Sveinung, and that they were both shape-changers. The brothers called Gunnstein out; he received them well and asked them to stay, and they accepted. He went in with them to the main room, and their outer clothes were taken from them. Supper was over, but they were offered good hospitality. Then Gunnstein leant forward in his chair and asked about their journey and their errand. Helgi answered readily, telling him what a dance Sveinung had led them during the day. And when he heard mention of Sveinung, Gunnstein asked most carefully how things had gone with them, and Helgi told him just what had happened.

In those days no one wore a knife in his belt; when men went out they had a knife hanging on a strap round the neck. Helgi drew his knife intending to eat. He took what was left on the dish; it was a short rib, so he took up his knife to cut the meat off it. Said Helgi, 'It's no exaggeration what they say about the sheep you raise in the Midfiords; this looks more like beef.'

Gunnstein answered nothing; he stretched out over the table and gripped Helgi's right arm above the wrist, crushing the hand so tightly that he lost all feeling in it, and the knife clattered down on to the table. Then Helgi threw down the short rib, and caught at his hand and looked up at Gunnstein. He saw that Gunnstein was as pale as a corpse with his hair standing up on his head.

Then Helgi said to Gunnstein, 'Are you going to attack us, you mad devil?'

Gunnstein answered, 'I shan't make a troll-change before you, but I shall keep hold of you till you tell me what you've done to my brother; and be quick about it.'

Helgi answered, 'Let go of me! I've not done anything to him, though I think he's a vile sorcerer too, and no better than you.'

'I think maybe you've the courage to tell me the truth,' said Gunnstein, 'but if you don't you'll have me to reckon with.' He let Helgi go then, but that hand was so numb that he could not feel his fingers. Helgi sprang up from the table, and they all went to the cross-benches and sat down. Not one of them took anything to eat and the food was taken away; the workmen went to bed. None of Helgi's men accepted any hospitality there; they lay down in their clothes and were there for the night.

And when a third of the night was past, Helgi went outside; the track was clear, although clouds were passing across the moon. He went in and roused his men and said there was good going all the way. They set off then, with no farewell to Gunnstein. They

went up on to the heath, and when they reached a farm called
Fannstod, and it is the last in Borgarfiord, the day was breaking.
They walked up the heath then, and Helgi was leading; it was very
hard going and he wanted to sit down and rest. He pushed his
spear away from him and the socket fell across his knees, and he
saw that the spearhead was all bloody.

. Then Helgi spoke. 'It's a true saying,' he said, ' "so near and yet
so far," and that has been the way of it here. Other people's advice
was worse than my own. The Norwegian must have been under
the boat. He got a wound from my spear and I do not know how
bad it is. We could have taken him if we'd done what I said.'

They answered, 'We'll go back at once and kill Sveinung if we
can't get the Norwegian.'

Helgi answered, 'He's deserved it, but it doesn't seem to me that
we can do much against those brothers. I think Sveinung must still
have a trick or two up his sleeve, and I don't believe we should
have the luck to outwit him when he was able to sneak Gunnar
away from under our very noses by his cunning. And now I must
say this, that I think Gunnar has few equals for courage and
endurance. So this time we must take our leave of him.'

Then Helgi stood up and walked on, and they did not stop till
they reached Arneidarstead. There they found Thorkel Geitisson,
and he asked how they had fared. Helgi told him everything just as
it had happened; Thorkel said that violence was growing all the
time, and that in dealing with those brothers they had to do with
no ordinary men. Thorkel said he had guarded his namesake in
Deep Hollow until midday, 'And when I set him free, he went
home to Njardvik.' And then they parted; Thorkel Geitisson went
home to Krossavik, and Helgi into Arneidarstead.

XX

The news of these events spread far and wide, and many thought
the Norwegian had had a narrow escape. Time passed and it was
not long before Sveinung left home taking the Norwegian with
him. They went up over the moor and did not stop until they
reached Mjovaness where they met Helgi Asbjarnarson. He
received Gunnar the Norwegian and took him in, and made him

go into his store-house, outside in the home meadow. No one but Helgi and Sveinung knew that he had sought shelter there, and he was there for the rest of the winter; most people thought that Gunnar was with Sveinung. Spring passed on till it was time for the Assembly which was held at Kidjafell, and Helgi Asbjarnarson had to consecrate it. He saw that he couldn't both go to consecrate the Assembly, and also guard Gunnar so that no one knew he was there. The evening before he was to ride away from home, he told Thordis Todda that Gunnar Thidrandi-killer was in his keeping.

'Now I want you to be responsible for him while I am away, and see that no one gets to know that he is here.'

'What a strange man you are, Helgi,' answered Thordis, 'if you think I am going to protect the man who has caused us so much loss of life. If I get my hands on him, I'll have him killed to avenge Thidrandi as I promised. It seems to me there's been a lot of violence among our kinsfolk, and it's not unlikely there's worse to come. Tomorrow I shall send the man to my brother Bjarni and he shall have that honour.'

'Do as you like,' said Helgi, 'I will give him to you. All the same you might bear in mind how much respect was paid you when you lived at home; you had only one gown and looked after the housework. Before I married you, you were treated no better than a slave as far as I could see. You might consider what you owe to me, because now people respect your opinion no less than mine. You are so looked up to now that almost every man will sit or stand as you wish. Now I'm telling you that as soon as you give this man up to Bjarni's axe you'll have to leave here and be sent north to Hof, to such honour as your brother Bjarni thinks fit to give you; and you'll never come into my house again as long as you live.'

'I don't care how you threaten me,' she answered, 'Bjarni won't keep me any worse than you do.'

They broke off then, and each kept to their own view of the matter.

Night passed by and in the morning men crowded to Helgi, and he had horses rounded up. Then he rode away with his company up on to the ridge and he consecrated the Assembly. When Helgi had gone Thordis went to the store-house and unlocked it. She went to Gunnar and gave him food, but didn't speak to him, and that day drew on to evening. By that time people in Mjovaness were preparing for supper and bed, and when they were at the table there was a knock at the door and someone went to open it; there were nearly eighty men outside. They called for Thordis and she went out; she recognized her brother Bjarni and gave him a joyous welcome and Bjarni was pleased at that. Their horses were taken care of and they were well entertained, and when supper was over they went to bed. Then Thordis went to Bjarni's bed and lay down along the edge of it; they began to talk for they had much to say to each other. However, at last Bjarni came round to saying, 'I've come here because I've heard that Gunnar has been here for some time. Now I know that Helgi can't look after him while he's at the Assembly, so he will be in your care now.'

She answered saying that this was not so; 'And I don't know why you should think I'd protect the man who has injured our family in such a way that nothing can ever compensate us.'

'I don't care what you say about this; I know he is in your house and I've come to you because I felt sure of your help. You can't keep the truth from me, and I know why you are trying to. Your husband must have warned you against giving Gunnar away, and threatened you, and brought up how miserable you were when you were at home. He must have threatened to drive you away in disgrace. However, if you come to Vapnafiord you shall have as much say in matters as here in the Fljotsdale district, if you respect my wishes in this affair.'

Thordis said she didn't know where Gunnar was and so had nothing to tell him.

'I can see that you're trying to hoodwink me but I could pretty well guess where he was if I wanted to search for him. Now I'll show you how anxious I am to get hold of the man. I have here in my pouch seven hundreds of silver,[1] and it is the best money there is. I'll give you this if you hand the man over to me.'

Thordis said, 'You are far less stingy with me now than when I was still at home, though I dare say you'd rather see me that much worse off. I would take the money if I knew where he was.'

---

[1] 840 ounces. The hundred here is the 'great' hundred, 120. This is the case in other references to 'hundreds of silver'.

Bjarni said, 'Then I'll tell you what will happen. Tomorrow I shall search your whole house for the most likely hiding-places. I think he is in your store-house and I shall drag him out and kill him before your eyes; and you won't like that.'

'He really won't be found here,' answered Thordis.

She turned now to her bed and was heavy at heart as might be expected. The household went to bed and as soon as they were asleep Thordis got up; she was still dressed. She roused her shepherd, telling him to come outside with her.

And when they were outside Thordis said, 'You are to go on an errand for me at once up to the Assembly place at Kidjafell. You must tell Helgi to come here as soon as he can and to bring many men with him. Say that guests have come whom I can't entertain in the proper fashion unless he is here; for I have no one I should show more honour to than my brother Bjarni. I know that he will come straight away. Ride hard and fast. If you carry out this errand faithfully I promise you you'll never have to herd sheep from now on as long as we are both alive.'

The shepherd took a horse and rode up on to the ridge and never stopped until he reached the Assembly. He rode to Helgi's booth and dismounted; he went inside and up to the place where Helgi lay resting. Helgi gave the servant a good welcome and asked for news, and he gave Helgi the message Thordis had given him; that was at dawn. Helgi got ready at once and summoned his men, telling them to round up the horses; he rode away from the Assembly with one hundred and eighty men and out along the ridges and so home to Mjovaness.

Early in the morning Bjarni got up at Mjovaness and had his men round up his horses with speed.

'I'm going off,' he said. Thordis went to him and asked him to have breakfast, 'before you ride'.

Bjarni said that because they were brother and sister he could not bring himself to ransack her house as if she were a thief, 'though you deserve such treatment. You are doing your very best to injure me. If I were to make a thorough search I should find him, because he must be where I told you last night.'

Brother and sister parted on bad terms for the time being, and after that Bjarni rode away with his men. They rode out along the lake and on their way they saw dust rising from the farm at Mjovaness.

Helgi was riding furiously and he came into the home meadows before Thordis had gone indoors. She turned to her husband and gave him a good welcome and told him about the talk she and Bjarni had had, and how it had turned out. 'I have set more store by you than by anyone else.'

Helgi thanked her for all her good-will. 'I knew that you were a good wife but I didn't know you were such a splendid woman. You have done much better than you said you would. Now I'll ride back to the Assembly if you think you are safe at home.' Then she told Helgi about Bjarni's offer and what he had said to her.

After that Helgi rode to the Assembly leaving Thordis in charge of the household at home. Bjarni rode back north to Hof but Helgi and Thordis kept Gunnar with them and looked after him well. He was there that summer and was well provided for, but was given his meals in secret.

XXI

The Droplaugarsons kept such good watch on Gunnar's ship that he was never able to reach it, or get hold of more than a few valuables. The Norwegians went abroad in the summer and came to Norway and said they did not know whether Gunnar would ever get back to Halogaland or not. Then they told all the news and described Gunnar's flight and how he had escaped.

That summer people rode to the Assembly; and Thorkel Geitisson put a price on Gunnar's head and laid a charge for his capture on all the chieftains. They all bound themselves to this, more especially the one Thorkel Geitisson had promised to befriend if he should succeed. That man was Thorkel Eyjolfsson who lived in the west and had married Gudrun Osvif's daughter. She was a friend of Helgi Asbjarnarson and they had formerly exchanged gifts, though Thorkel Eyjolfsson knew nothing about it.

When summer was over, Helgi had three horses shod and got a man to escort Gunnar; he sent him north over Modrudalesheath and north along the upper road to Myvatn, and then west into the country until he came to Helgafell. He was sent there to Gudrun, Osvif's daughter, for support and safe-keeping, with plenty of tokens to show that she was to welcome him gladly, keep him there at first for the winter, and get him abroad the next summer. It turned out well, for Thorkel was not at home; he had promised Thorkel Geitisson to kill Gunnar if he caught him, but he had gone out to the islands to fetch dried fish.

Gudrun gave Gunnar a very kind reception. His travelling companion made only a short stay there and rode straight back to the East Fiords. Gudrun sent fine presents to Helgi Asbjarnarson.

The son of Gudrun and Thorkel was called Gellir; he was young, and most accomplished and a great seagoing trader. He came to the mouth of the Lax river that summer, and was staying with his father and mother at Helgafell.

When Gunnar had been there one night, Thorkel came home late in the evening. There was a big crowd there and fires were made for them and their outer clothes taken off them. People were going through the main room to the fires, and Thorkel saw a man in a blue tunic and grey hooded cloak coming forward; he was not very tall but very strongly built and had a gleaming axe in his hand. This man had fair hair, regular features and a handsome appearance. Thorkel asked the valiant-looking man who he was; he told him his name was Gest.

Thorkel stared at the man for a while and said, 'You are remarkably like the man they called Gunnar who is nicknamed Thidrandi-killer; he has been in the East Fiords for some time. But where is your home and where do you intend to go?'

He was lost for words and did not reply.

Thorkel went on, 'It seems to me that you are not the man you claim to be, and I am sure I can tell you your name and business.'

'If you're right about this,' answered Gunnar, 'what will you do?'

Thorkel replied, 'You'll soon find out.' He jumped up and seized a sword which was lying on the seat and was called Skofnung and which was later lost with him in Breidafiord. He drew the sword at once and jumped over the fire and struck at Gunnar. Gunnar swung his axe above his head and Thorkel's blow missed the man but struck the neck of the axe blade so hard that the sword stuck there.

Gunnar sprang back and jerked up the axe.

People ran into the main room and told Gudrun what was going on in the kitchen. She came forward and begged her husband Thorkel to calm down; 'You'd better not hurt him unless you want us to part from this very day. Gunnar was sent me by friends for safe-keeping and protection. I shall take care of him as if he were my own son until ships sail from Iceland in the summer, and if anyone so much as pulls a hair from his head I'll pay them out for such cruelty as best I can. Those who have experienced it say that it is no laughing matter to incur my wrath. I'll stop at nothing if I hear that anyone has hurt him. You'd better leave him quite alone; he will be safe in my kindly care.'

Thorkel answered, 'You often want your own way, Gudrun; and there's no peace till you get it. We're often made to look small if you start meddling.' Thorkel soon quietened down and stopped being angry. Gunnar stayed there that winter and was well provided for.

XXII

It is said that once at the Removal Days,[1] when Gudrun and Thorkel had gone to bed, Thorkel asked, 'What do you want me to do with this Gunnar of yours?'

'I'll soon tell you,' said Gudrun. 'There's a ship lying up in the mouth of the Lax that my son Gellir sailed here last summer. I'll have it loaded there, and made ready for a voyage abroad this summer. I'll fit it out with goods and all its tackle and give it to Gunnar, and Gellir shall stay here and not go abroad this summer.'

Thorkel said nothing against this. 'You are very domineering, Gudrun; I suppose it will turn out as it often does, that there will be little peace till you get your way.' They stopped talking then and the night passed by.

Next morning Thorkel was up very early. The ship was launched and a large and excellent cargo put on board; husband and wife spared no expense in furnishing it in fine style. And when

[1] These were four days in May when people in Iceland used to change their farms.

the ship was quite ready they led Gunnar to it, and gave him the ship with yard and rigging and many valuables. Gunnar thanked them for this gift and for all the honour they had shown him and they parted very good friends.

Gunnar put out to sea as soon as he got a fair wind; he had a very good voyage, made land where he intended to, and that was where his father had settled before him. Gunnar was the son of a 'hersir'[1] and ruled over Halogaland. He was given a great reception there because people almost thought that he had got back from the dead. Both in Iceland and elsewhere many people declared and affirmed that no man with such heroes at his heels had ever made such a narrow escape. The following summer Gunnar loaded the ship with many valuables and sent it out to Iceland with gifts for Thorkel and Gudrun Osvif's daughter, and those others whom he felt he had good reason to reward. The ship came to the mouth of the Lax and Gellir took it and sailed it for a long time afterwards in trading voyages. But Gunnar stayed at his home in Halogaland and doesn't come much into the story after this.

XXIII

A man called Hallstein lived at North Vidivellir in Fljotsdale; he has been mentioned earlier in the story. He was a big man and a most trustworthy farmer. He had two sons, Sighvat and Snorri, who were highly accomplished and who stayed alternately at home with their father and with Hrafnkel Thorisson. They were very self-assertive men and were always contending with people, enjoying much support from Hrafnkel who was the most powerful chieftain of his day. For some years Hallstein had various women in charge of his home, but he found this most inconvenient.

It is said that one spring he rode down to Bersastead; Bersi gave him a very good welcome and asked why he had come.

Hallstein replied, 'I want you to ride over to Arneidarstead with me. For a long time I've been living in great discomfort and now I want to marry, and to do so with your backing.'

---

[1] Chieftain next in rank to an earl in early Norway.

'Who is the woman?' asked Bersi.

Hallstein answered, 'Her name is Droplaug and she is the daughter of Bjorgolf.'

'I don't want you to do that,' said Bersi, 'for I think you'll find you can't manage her. She is a most accomplished woman, but I doubt if she is everyone's match. I think you would be quite incompatible because she is a very haughty woman and of good family, whereas you are from a small farmer's family and are contented with little. You are a very wealthy man, but you'd be taking on more than you can cope with. I advise you, as I would others, to use foresight and judgement in looking for a suitable partner. Moreover your sons are boisterous; Helgi and his brother are known to be somewhat impetuous, and if you and Droplaug don't agree then your sons will find the brothers getting on top of them. I shouldn't have expected you to aim so high, and I don't think you'll find your journey is welcomed. I have been without a wife for a long time and have often been urged to ask Droplaug for her hand, but I never thought it would suit me to marry her; I would rather live alone for a time. I can't encourage you, but all the same, do as you like.'

Hallstein answered, 'It's a true saying that one shouldn't trust anyone, because the one you trust most can disappoint you most. Now I never thought, Bersi, that you would spurn me like this, my reputation being at stake. I've been friends with you for a long time and believed in you almost like a god, but the more I need you, the more you fail me.'

Bersi said, 'It's an old saying that he who warns is not to be blamed. Now I've told you my opinion, but I'll go with you if you like. What you do is your responsibility, but I'm telling you the truth when I warn you that you are the one who will most regret taking this step.'

Hallstein answered, 'Be that as it may, I'm going ahead with it.'

Then they, Bersi and Hallstein, rode out along the countryside until they came to Arneidarstead where, as usual, they were given a pleasant welcome and they stayed there that night.

In the morning Bersi went to Droplaug and her sons and said he had pressing business with them. They began to talk and Bersi related his errand.

Droplaug and her sons were slow to reply, but Bersi asked them not to take too long about this affair. 'I ask you as honourable men to say what you really think.'

Helgi answered, 'I do not think that Droplaug and Hallstein will suit each other very well. Now I want her to speak for herself, and I'll agree with what she decides.'

'It is clear', said Droplaug, 'that Hallstein has seen we're short of ready money. For a long time we have been using the money acquired and owned by your father Thorvald. Now a great deal has gone in general upkeep of the farm; every autumn we have to lay out much money for our housekeeping, and in the spring we need to spend heavily on our milking herd. However, I should not like to be less hospitable than I have been. Now in my opinion we haven't much in the way of livestock but we don't lack land. In a word this is my offer, Hallstein: I am to go up into Vidivellir with you and take possession of half your goods, bringing no money from here except a few valuables, because I want my sons to enjoy their patrimony. Further, I want my sons to be joint heirs along with the children I bear you. I'll never live long enough to repay the husband I married for the good-will he showed me. Above all things I should very much like my sons to enjoy whatever will be of use to them.'

Her sons told her to settle her own affairs and said they reckoned their own wealth would last out their time.

Droplaug said Hallstein should now choose whether to marry her on these terms or not. Hallstein showed no hesitation and the business was settled. Droplaug was then betrothed to Hallstein and after that he and Bersi rode home.

XXIV

This news spread throughout the district and the sons of Hallstein heard it like everyone else. Then they went home to Vidivellir and having taken over what their mother had left them, they shared it between them, took their money and went away. After that a feast was prepared and people were invited to it, and nearly all the chieftains came. But Droplaug's sons showed so little respect to Hallstein that they would not accept her invitation; Hrafnkel was not there, nor was Helgi Asbjarnarson. It was a splendid feast and a great success. Afterwards Droplaug took over the housekeeping and the supervision of everything indoors and out, and she was no less hospitable than before.

The Droplaug brothers took over their farm, engaged a woman as housekeeper and went on showing their usual hospitality.

Hallstein and Droplaug did not get on very well together, but not badly either; Hallstein's sons, however, disliked Droplaug so much that they never came to see their father.

And the first year they came together Droplaug became pregnant, and time passed until, in due course, she gave birth to a child. It was a boy, and he was sprinkled with water and given the name of Bjorgolf after his grandfather on his mother's side. The boy grew up and promised very well and they loved him much, for he developed early in every way.

XXV

The Droplaugarsons came to see their mother regularly, and on the way they always made a long stay at Bersastead. There was one thing about Bersi that Helgi did not like at all, and that was his devotion to the gods; he had much faith in the gods and made many sacrifices. Bersi thought Helgi abused the gods as he did because he was so unwilling to believe in them.

Helgi said, 'Nothing you do strikes me as being so foolish as this, that you show veneration for those man-made idols which are both blind and deaf and dumb, for I understand that they are unable to do any good to themselves or to anyone else. I am much more uncivil to you than I would be otherwise, because I alone know how I abhor the gods. In every other matter you give me the greatest support.'

Bersi replied, 'You would be the wisest of all the men now growing up in the whole of Iceland if you trusted in their mercy.'

Helgi answered, 'May I never be in such straits as to look for help from those devils who are evil through and through.' And so they parted.

Droplaug and Hallstein got on pretty well together for seven years. All the same, the longer they were together the worse things grew between them. Although there was plenty of money, Hallstein being very well off, great uneasiness was felt in the house. Droplaug often sent her sons word that they should come to share out the money with Hallstein, but they kept on putting it off.

XXVI

One midwinter day it happened that a messenger came from Vidivellir to Arneidarstead to say that Droplaug wanted her sons to come and see her as soon as possible. They got the message but did not hurry to set out, and the week wore on. Then another messenger came on the same errand as the first.

Helgi told the man to go home – 'I'll come when I think the time is ripe' – and the messenger returned with nothing done.

That winter the weather was harsh and the tracks were bad throughout the countryside. One morning Helgi was afoot very early and told his brother Grim to get up. Grim got up and dressed, and they went out. There was a wind blowing off the sea; there was a clear sky, but a blizzard up in the mountains and a terribly hard frost. Helgi went south over the gully and down from the hill slopes; but when they came on to the ice they found it very hard going. It grew dark, a great snowstorm came on, and the snow began to drift in the wind.

Helgi spoke up. 'It's much worse going than I thought it would be,' he said; 'we shall have to cross the heath and go up along by the farms, because I think it will be easier that way.' Then the weather grew very bad, with a fearsome blizzard; the wind went round to the north and blew off the heath. The brothers walked all day until it grew very dark. Then at last they came to a steep gully and crossed it. 'What gully is this?' asked Grim.

Helgi answered, 'I think it must be Oeroefagil between Bersastead and Skrida, south of Bersastead, because I think it has been more solid underfoot coming down from the heath.'

Grim said that could not be. 'Because it is still bad going, however, I think it would be wiser for us to go down to the farmland; we'll be certain of a night's lodging if we come to a farm.'

They went down from the mountain and found the way very bad, and when they came to level ground they could not see any farms and had no idea where they were going. They kept on walking along through the countryside until they came to a gravel bank that had been swept clear of snow, and followed it. When they least expected it they lost their footing and plunged down an overhanging mass of snow, and they burst out laughing. It was wet where they fell down. They were dressed in belted breeks and over them fur cloaks fastened at the wrists, and they wore swords, and carried stout staves in their hands; they always dressed like this for an expedition. They thrust down with their iron-tipped staves and struck ice.

Grim asked Helgi if he knew at all where they were.

Helgi replied, 'Far from it. I do not know of any ice hereabouts except on Lagarfljot, nor any gravel banks that I can think of.' Helgi said he did not know where they had got to. They pushed on vigorously however, and came off the ice and over a barren rocky place, where they saw a blackness in the storm before them; it was a big earthwork, and stood as high as Helgi. They walked round the earthwork, which was circular, and found a strongly built barred gate in front of them.

Helgi said, 'You must know where we are now.'

'No, I don't,' replied Grim, 'quite the contrary; I've never come to this place before that I can remember.'

'I have though,' said Helgi; 'I know for certain where we are. This is my foster-father Bersi's temple. There are springs above it; we came to them before, on the ice, and this is what has happened to us.' That place is now called Bersi's Springs.

Grim said, 'Let's get away as fast as we can.'

'No,' said Helgi, 'I shall go in, because I want to see what sort of a house the gods have here.'

Then he went to the gateway and struck the lock with his sword-hilt and smashed it. They went up to the temple and broke it open; then they went inside.

Then Grim said, 'You're doing wrong, brother, acting in such a high-handed manner, and doing so much damage everywhere here. I'm sure Bersi your foster-father will be angry if he gets to know about it.'

Helgi answered, 'I want to see what sort of hosts these fiends will be to us, because I doubt if I shall ever be in greater need than I am now, and if they don't behave well now, they won't on another occasion.'

Then Helgi went into the temple; it was light inside, but the light cast no shadow. All the walls were hung with tapestry and both benches were occupied; the whole place glowed with silver and gold. The gods stared straight ahead and did not welcome those who had come. Frey and Thor sat side by side on the high-seat of the lower bench.

Helgi turned to them and said, 'There the two of you sit, devil's limbs as you are; no doubt your worshippers look on you both as honourable chieftains. Now, if you want us brothers to believe in you as others do, stand up, and invite us in, for it's bad weather outside. If you will agree to this, we brothers will trust in you as others do; but if you show arrogance, and refuse to help us, then we shan't show you any respect.'

They showed arrogance, and were silent.

Then Helgi crossed the floor to where Frigg and Freya were seated. He spoke the same words to them, saying he would be gentle with them if they would give him better entertainment.

Grim said, 'Please don't talk to these devils any more, but let us go away.'

Helgi said, 'I'm not going to be like most people and attack at the weakest point.' Then he went for Thor and his companions, knocking them off their seats. He took away their clothes, and went from one to another of the gods, stripping them of all their clothing and treasures, and tumbling them down from their seats on to the floor. He carried everything into a corner and covered it all up so that nothing should be spoiled.

'This is a poor joke,' said Grim, 'and even if they are nobody's favourites you'll make an enemy of our foster-father Bersi. This is an ill deed.'

Helgi answered, 'And I don't think I've ever in my life done a better deed than this. It was the gods who confused the path before me today, because this is the first time in my life that I've ever lost my way.'

Helgi went out and left the temple open; and now the snow was whirled round about inside the whole building. Helgi and Grim then turned down to the river and up along the headland until they came to Vidivellir, and by that time it was nightfall. The people there welcomed them gladly and they stayed for a night or two. Then the weather changed for the better, and Droplaug had a long talk with her sons, but no one else knew what they said to one another. Afterwards they went home, when they thought. . . .

DROPLAUGARSONASAGA OR THE DROPLAUGARSONS

I

There was a man called Ketil, nicknamed Thrym [Rowdy], who lived at Husastead in Skridudale; he had a brother called Atli Graut [Porridge]. They lived together and were well off, travelling often to other countries with goods for sale. They became very wealthy; they were the sons of Thidrandi. One spring Ketil made his ship ready for a voyage in Reydarfiord, where it had been laid up, and afterwards he set sail. They were at sea for a very long time, making Konungahella in the autumn, and there they beached the ship. Later on Ketil bought himself horses and, taking eleven men with him, rode east to Jamtaland. He went to a man called Vethorm who was a prominent chieftain and a good friend of Ketil's. He was the son of Ronald son of Ketil the Monstrous; he had three brothers, Grim, Guttorm and Ormar, all great fighting men who spent the summer raiding and stayed with Vethorm in the winter. Ketil was there for the winter with his men. There were two stranger women in Vethorm's household, one worked away as hard as she could, while the other sat sewing, and she was the elder. The younger woman's work was good, but she got little thanks for it and often wept. Ketil noticed this, and one day, before he had been there very long, this woman went to the river to wash clothes and afterwards she washed her hair; it was beautiful, she had a lot of it and it suited her well.

Ketil knew where she was and went there and spoke to her, asking, 'Who are you?'

'My name is Arneid,' she answered.

'What family do you come from?' asked Ketil.

'I don't think that's any business of yours,' she said.

He insisted on knowing and ordered her to tell him.

Then she answered, weeping, 'My father's name was Asbjorn and he was called Skerjablesi. He ruled in the Hebrides, and was earl of the islands after Tryggvi's death. Then afterwards Vethorm raided there, with all his brothers in eighteen ships. They came one night to my father's house and burned him in it with all the menfolk, but the women were let out. Afterwards they brought my mother Sigrid and me here, but they sold all the other women as slaves. And now Guttorm is the ruler of the islands.'

Then they broke off their talk, but the next day Ketil asked Vethorm, 'Will you sell Arneid to me?' Vethorm replied, 'Since we are friends I'll let you have her for a half hundred of silver.[1] Ketil then offered to pay for her keep, 'for she is not to work'. Vethorm said he would allow her the same provision as other members of his household.

That summer Vethorm's brothers Grim and Ormar came home; they had been raiding in Sweden during the summer and each of them had his merchant-ship laden with valuables. They stayed with Vethorm that winter, but in the spring the brothers made their ships ready for Iceland, intending to sail later with Ketil. When they were standing off Vik [Oslo fiord] Arneid asked Ketil for leave to go ashore to gather herself some nuts, along with the other woman who was on board. He gave her leave and told her not to go far, so they went ashore and came to a ridge, when it began to rain heavily. Arneid said to the other woman, 'Go to the ship and ask Ketil to come to me because I feel ill.' She did so and Ketil came to Arneid, by himself. She greeted him and said, 'I've found charcoal here.' They dug in the sand and found a chest full of silver which they carried to the ship. Then Ketil offered to take her with the money to her kinsfolk, but she chose to stay with him. After that they put out to sea, and the ships got separated.

Ketil brought his ship into Reydarfiord, laid it up, and then travelled home to his house at Husastead. A fortnight later Ormar sailed into Reydarfiord and Ketil invited him home after his ship was laid up. That summer Grim brought his ship into the harbour

[1] 60 ounces.

in Eyr which is called Knarrasund, and he stayed the winter with a man called Thorkel. The following spring Grim took the land which was afterwards called Grimsness and lived at Burfell all his life.

II

Now we must take up the story when Ketil Thrym bought land west of the lake called Lagarfljot, and he lived there afterwards; that farm is called Arneidarstead.

At the Spring Assembly Ketil bought for Ormar land a bit further out from the lake, where Ormar lived till his old age; it was called Ormarsstead. Next Ketil bought a godord for himself, paying for it in silver, but before that he and his brother Graut Atli had shared out their money. Atli bought land east of the lake, above Hallormsstead; it is now called Atlavik and he lived there till his old age and there are still remains of sheep-pens there. After this Ketil married Arneid as she was a most splendid woman. They had a son called Thidrandi who was a tall, handsome man; Ketil did not live long and Thidrandi took over the property and godord after his father.

There was a man called Havar son of Bersi, who was known as Bersi the Wise. He lived in Vallaness and had a wife and two children: a son Bersi[1] and a daughter Yngvild. Yngvild was considered a very good match, and Thidrandi asked for her hand and she was married to him.

A man called Egil had taken all Nordrfiord and built a house there which is called Ness. He was the son of Guttorm and called the Red Egil; he was married and had one daughter called Ingibjorg. Bersi Havarson asked for her and she married him and with her went Nessland. Thidrandi and Yngvild had many children: one of their sons was called Ketil and another Thorvald. Their daughter Joreid was married to Hall of the Side; another daughter was called Hallkatla, and Geitir Lytingsson who lived at Krossavik in Vapnafiord married her. The third daughter was called Groa; she lived up north at Eyvindara and her son was called Bard.

[1] Later called Ozurarson.

When Ketil and Thorvald were grown up their father Thidrandi took ill and died; they inherited after him but did not get on together over sharing the property. Thorvald was tall and strong, a reserved and determined man, powerful in his own district. Ketil was a cheery fellow and much involved in lawsuits. They divided the property between them, Thorvald taking Arneidarstead while Ketil had the godord, lived at Njardvik, and was a great chieftain.

There was a man called Thorgrim who lived at Gil[jar], north in Jokulsdale. He had a wife, and one daughter who was called Droplaug: she was beautiful and most accomplished. Thorvald asked for Droplaug and that marriage came about; they had two sons, the elder called Helgi and the younger Grim, and there was one year between them. Thorvald did not live to be old, and died. Droplaug, however, went on living at Arneidarstead with her sons. Helgi was a tall man, strong and handsome, a cheery self-assertive fellow who gave no thought to the farm; he was very well skilled in arms. Grim was a tall man, very strong, reserved and moderate, and a very good farmer. The brothers exercised themselves in every kind of sport; they excelled all the young men in the neighbourhood with their exploits so that none could be found to match them.

III

There was a man called Bersi who lived at Bersastead; he was the son of Ozur and had a son called Holmstein, who lived at South Vidivellir and was married to Aslaug the daughter of Thorir and sister of Hrafnkel the Godi. A man called Hallstein the Broaddaler lived at North Vidivellir. He was both rich and popular. His wife was called Thorgerd and they had three sons, Thorod, Thorkel and Eindridi. A man called Thorgeir lived at Hrafnkelsstead. Helgi Asbjarnarson lived at Oddsstead above the river Hafr; he had a godord and was married to Droplaug the daughter of Bersi the Wise. They had many children. A man called Hrafnkel, the nephew of Helgi Asbjarnarson, lived at Hafrsa. He was a young man; he and Helgi Asbjarnarson held the godord in common, but Helgi acted as Godi. At that time a man called An the Clown lived at Gunnlaugarstead north of Mjovaness. There was a man called

Ozur who lived below Ass to the west of the lake and he was a kinsman of Helgi Asbjarnarson. Hjarrandi was the name of a man who lived at Ongulsa east of the lake at Vellir; he was married to Helgi Asbjarnarson's daughter Thorkatla.[1] Ozur is said to have been an able man who was often employed in lawsuits. There was a man called Bjorn the White who lived at Myrar, to the west of the river Geitdale, and he was married to another of Helgi Asbjarnarson's daughters.

It was the custom in those days to take food to women who were resting in bed after childbirth, and it so happened that Droplaug went to see her mother Ingibjorg at Bersastead, and two slaves accompanied her; they travelled on a sledge drawn by two oxen. Droplaug stayed there for one night, because the following night there was to be a feast at Oddsstead, and this was a short time before the Spring Assembly. They made for home, driving over the ice, and when they reached Hallormsstead the slaves got on to the sledge, as the oxen knew their way home. But when they came to the creek to the south of Oddsstead, both oxen fell through a hole in the ice and they were all drowned there; since then it has been called Slaves' Creek. Helgi's shepherd told him the news when he was alone, and Helgi told him not to tell anyone else. Afterwards Helgi went to the Spring Assembly, and there he sold Oddsstead and bought Mjovaness. He moved house there, thinking he would the sooner forget Droplaug's death. Some time later he asked for the hand of Thordis Todda, Spike-Helgi's daughter, and she was married to him.

There was a man called Thorir who lived at Myness, out to the east of the lake: he was a married man and very sensible. Staying with him was a man called Thorgrim, nicknamed Dungbeetle. There was a man called Thorfin who worked for hire in the summer, but in the winter when he had no job he travelled as a pedlar. In the autumn he was staying with Thorir for the night, and was sitting by the fire among the household. Much of the talk turned on the women in the neighbourhood, and which were most notable. They agreed that Droplaug of Arneidarstead far surpassed most women. Then Thorgrim said, 'She might, if she'd been satisfied with her husband.' They replied, 'We've never heard it

[1] She was illegitimate.

doubted', and at that Thorir came over to them, and told them to hold their tongues at once.

Night passed away, and Thorfin went off, and came to Arneidarstead and let Droplaug know everything Thorir's workmen had said. She took no notice at first, except that she kept silence. One morning Helgi asked his mother what was the matter. She told the brothers how Thorgrim Dungbeetle had slandered her, 'But you won't avenge this disgrace, or any other I have to bear.' They pretended not to hear what she was saying. At that time Helgi was thirteen and Grim twelve.

A little later they got ready to leave the house, saying they were going to visit their aunt Groa at Eyvindara; they went there over the ice and stayed one night. In the morning they got up early and Groa asked them what they were going to do. They answered, 'We're going to hunt ptarmigan.' They went to Myness, met a woman there and asked where the farmer was. She said he had gone out with seven men to the sandbanks. 'What are the workmen doing?' asked Helgi. She said, 'Thorgrim Dungbeetle and Asmund have gone on to the island to fetch hay.' Then Helgi and Grim left the farmstead and followed the Jarnsida brook down the ridge and went after them on to the island. Asmund was up on the stack and saw them coming, and recognized the brothers; he and Thorgrim unhitched the draught-horse from the sledge. Thorgrim meant to ride home but, just as he was mounting, Helgi shot a spear into his middle and he fell dead at once. Asmund was terrified and set off home with the draught-horse. The brothers walked off and back to Eyvindara; Groa asked them what they had caught. 'We've caught one dungbeetle,' replied Helgi. 'Although you make light of this killing,' she said, 'Thorir is a very important man, and you must go home now to Arneidarstead.' They did so, and kept a big crowd of men there.

IV

Thorir came home in the evening and heard the news, and said that he was not going to shoulder the responsibility for this incident, since Thorgrim was a freed slave of Helgi Asbjarnarson's. Then he went to see Helgi Asbjarnarson and told him about the killing. 'I reckon you have to take up the suit.' Helgi agreed, and after that Thorir went home.

On one occasion Droplaug had a talk with her sons and said, 'I am going to send you to Geitir at Krossavik in Vapnafiord.' They left home going west over the heath, and when they had walked about a league a violent snowstorm came on so that they couldn't tell where they were going until they came up against the wall of a house, and they went round it sunwise. Then they found a door and Helgi recognized it as the heathen temple of Bersi the Wise. They turned away from it at once and went back home, reaching Arneidarstead when two-thirds of the night had passed. The storm lasted for a fortnight however, and folk thought that a very long time. Bersi the Wise said it did so because the Droplaugarsons had gone sunwise round his temple, and moreover that they had not declared Dungbeetle's killing according to law, and the gods were angered by that. Afterwards Bersi went to see the brothers and they declared the killing, and then travelled north to Geitir in Krossavik.

The next spring Thorkel Geitisson, Grim and Helgi went to the Krakaloek Spring Assembly in Fljotsdale. There they met Helgi Asbjarnarson and settled the suit for the killing of Thorgrim with money paid by Thorkel. But Helgi Droplaugarson did not like it that money should be paid for Dungbeetle's killing and he considered the slander to be unavenged. The brothers stayed on in Krossavik and Helgi learned law from Thorkel. Helgi was involved in a great many lawsuits, especially in those against thingmen[1] of Helgi Asbjarnarson. The brothers often went to stay with their mother.

Eindridi Hallsteinsson had gone abroad, and had been captured in Ireland where he was held in fetters. His brothers Thorkel and Thorod heard of this and went abroad and freed him; afterwards they sailed to Iceland. Hallstein's wife had died by then and he asked for Droplaug and married her, but Helgi said this was not with his consent; afterwards Droplaug went to live with Hallstein at Vidivellir.

The brothers Helgi and Grim, and ten men with them, went out

---

[1] A chieftain's followers and members of an Assembly.

to Tongue to visit the farmer called Ingjald Nidgestson. He had a daughter called Helga, and Grim asked for her, and she married him. Afterwards Ingjald sold his land and bought half Arneidarstead, and he and his son-in-law Grim lived there together. Helgi Droplaugarson, however, was time and time about in Krossavik, or with Grim and Ingjald.

Hrafnkel laid claim to the godord which he held along with his kinsman Helgi Asbjarnarson, but met with no success, so he went to see Holmstein at Vidivellir and asked him for help. Holmstein said, 'I can't go against Helgi Asbjarnarson because he was married to my sister, but I advise you to go to Helgi Droplaugarson for backing, and I'll get my thingmen to support you.' Then Hrafnkel went tó visit Helgi Droplaugarson and asked for his help. Helgi said, 'It seems to me that Holmstein ought to think more of the fact that he is your sister's husband, than of the past.' But Hrafnkel begged Helgi to help him. Helgi said, 'I advise you to go in a week's time to Gunnlaugarstead to meet An the Clown, and tell him what a fine fellow you think him.' Now An and Helgi Asbjarnarson were good friends because An had often given Helgi valuable presents. 'You must ask An how highly he thinks Helgi esteems him, and butter him up with every word, and if he likes that, ask him if he has ever been nominated to a court for Helgi Asbjarnarson's godord. If he says no, tell him he would do better if he gave Helgi Asbjarnarson his stud-horse so as to gain the privilege of being called to appear in court.' After that they parted. Some time later Hrafnkel went to see An and told him what Helgi had prescribed, and An said he would try this. Then Hrafnkel rode home.

In the spring people went to the Spring Assembly and then Helgi Asbjarnarson nominated An the Clown as a member of the court. It was to be kept quiet because An had given Helgi Asbjarnarson no fewer than seven stud-horses, and when An took his seat in the court Helgi Asbjarnarson had a felt hood put over his head to conceal who he was, and told him to keep quiet. Then Hrafnkel went to the court along with the Droplaugarsons and a great crowd of men; Helgi Droplaugarson walked up to the bench where An was sitting and jerked the hood off his head with his sword-hilt and flung it away, asking who was sitting there. An told him who he was. Helgi asked, 'Who cited you to the court of this godord?' An replied, 'Helgi Asbjarnarson did.' Then Helgi Droplaugarson told Hrafnkel to name witnesses and declared Helgi Asbjarnarson to have forfeited his godord, and declared all his lawsuits to be null and void since he had appointed An to the court. There was a great tumult then and the crowd got ready to fight, but Holmstein went among them and tried to get a settlement. It was agreed that Hrafnkel should have the godord that Helgi had enjoyed for as long as he and Helgi had owned it, and after that Hrafnkel and Helgi were to share it in common, also that Helgi was to support Hrafnkel in all his lawsuits at Assemblies and meetings of men when he needed help. Helgi Droplaugarson said to Hrafnkel, 'Now I consider that I have helped you.' He said that that was so, and then people went home from the Assembly.

V

Later that year it was a very bad season, and many sheep died; Thorgeir, a farmer at Hrafnkelsstead, lost many of his.

There was a man called Thord who lived at Geirolfseyr west of the Skridudale river. He was well off and had fostered one of Helgi Asbjarnarson's children. Thorgeir went there and bought fifty ewes from him, giving wadmal[1] for them; he had little profit from these animals for they strayed away from him. In the autumn Thorgeir went himself to look for his sheep and found eighteen of them in pens at Geirolfseyr, and they had been milked. He asked some women who had ordered this to be done, and they said it was Thord. Then he went to see Thord and asked him for compensation; he spoke with restraint, asking Thord to do one thing or the other, either to give him an equal number of two-year-old wethers, or to feed the ewes through the winter. But Thord refused to do either, saying he would gain little by having fostered Helgi Asbjarnarson's child if he had to pay for such a thing as this.

Afterwards Thorgeir went to see Helgi Asbjarnarson and told

---

[1] Plain woollen stuff.

him about it. Helgi said, 'I want Thord to compensate you, and you have a just case; tell him what I say.' Thorgeir went to see Thord but to no purpose. Then he went to Helgi Droplaugarson and asked him to take up the suit, 'and if you do so I'd like you to have the money'. On these terms Helgi Droplaugarson took up the suit. In the spring he went to Geirolfseyr and summoned Thord to the Althing, declaring that Thord had thievishly hidden the ewes and had stolen the animals' milk. Afterwards the suit came up at the Althing, and Helgi Droplaugarson and Thorkel Geitisson had a very large number of men with them including Ketil of Njardvik, but Helgi Asbjarnarson had not numbers sufficient to quash the suit. Then men urged them to come to terms, but Helgi Droplaugarson refused to accept anything but the right to assess compensation for himself and he fixed the fine at as many cows as the ewes that had been milked by Thord. They separated then, according to the terms set, and Helgi Droplaugarson thought the suit had gone most satisfactorily.

VI

There was a man called Sveinung who lived at Bakki in Borgarfiord. He was the son of Thorir, a tall man, strong and capable, and a friend of Helgi Droplaugarson's. The following year Helgi Droplaugarson stayed a long time with Sveinung in Borgarfiord.

There was a man called Thorstein who lived at Desjarmyr in Borgarfiord; his wife was called Thordis, and she was a near kinswoman of the Droplaugarsons. There was a man called Bjorn who lived at Snotruness in Borgarfiord; he was married, but he was not content with his wife alone. Bjorn was the foster-father of Helgi Asbjarnarson and he was always going to Desjarmyr to talk with Thorstein's wife Thordis. At this time Thorstein had grown infirm with age, yet was still a fine man; Thordis had married him for his money.

Thorstein spoke to Helgi Droplaugarson one day and asked him to try to persuade Bjorn to leave off coming to visit Thordis. Helgi was reluctant, but said he would try some time or other.

On one occasion Bjorn went to Desjarmyr by night; Helgi and

Sveinung came to meet him and Helgi said, 'Bjorn, I wish you would stop coming to visit Thordis; it's not to your credit to annoy an old man. Do as I ask you now, and another time I'll do the same for you.' Bjorn did not answer, but went on his way.

Another time Helgi met Bjorn coming away from Desjarmyr, and asked him quietly to stop going there, but Bjorn said, 'Fault-finding won't do you any good.' As the upshot of this affair Thordis became pregnant, and this was known throughout the countryside.

Helgi took up the suit for Thorstein and demanded compensation from Bjorn who said he would not pay, nor would he accept any responsibility in the matter. Then Helgi struck Bjorn his death-blow, declaring him an outlaw because there was a true charge against him. The next night Helgi and two others carried Bjorn to an offshore skerry and buried him there; since then it has been called Bjarnarsker.

Men were sent to Helgi Asbjarnarson at Mjovaness, and it was thought that Bjorn's wife had the right to expect him to take up the case. That spring, after the slaying, Helgi Asbjarnarson went to Borgarfiord to prepare his case, but he did not find Bjorn's body. Afterwards he accused Helgi Droplaugarson of having concealed a dead man and sunk him in the sea, instead of burying him in the ground.

Helgi Asbjarnarson brought his suit for outlawry to the Assembly; Helgi Droplaugarson had prepared a suit for adultery to bring to the Althing. Now both suits came up to the Althing for judgement together. Then Helgi Asbjarnarson called on the defendant to begin his pleading. Helgi Droplaugarson went to the court with a great following, and named witnesses to the effect that the whole of Helgi Asbjarnarson's suit was null and void, because there were three men who had seen Bjorn buried in the ground. Sveinung and two men with him took an oath[1] on the altar ring that they had seen Bjorn buried in the ground, and so Helgi Asbjarnarson's suit was quashed. Helgi Droplaugarson wanted to make Bjorn an outlaw, but Helgi Asbjarnarson offered money instead, and Helgi Droplaugarson was to decide the

---

[1] In heathen times men swore by the altar ring in the same way as later they swore by the cross or the Bible.

amount. He claimed 100 aurir,[1] which were current at that time, as compensation, and so they parted.

VII

Some years later Helgi Droplaugarson came to his mother and his step-father Hallstein from the Autumn Assembly at North Vidivellir; he had not been there since their marriage. Droplaug asked her husband Hallstein to invite Helgi to stay for the winter. He, however, replied, 'I don't much want to do that; I'd rather give him some oxen or horses,' but because she insisted he invited Helgi to stay, and he accepted.

Hallstein had a slave called Thorgils. One morning a fortnight later, Droplaug, Helgi and the slave had a long talk together, and no one else knew what they talked about. In the winter Thorgils worked with sheep in the fenced field at the south end of the farm; he was a good worker. A great deal of hay had been carted there.

One day Thorgils came to Hallstein and asked him to come and look over his hay and sheep. Hallstein came to the barn and was making for the window when Thorgils struck at him with Helgi Droplaugarsons's axe; only one blow was needed to kill him. Helgi was up the fellside with his horses; he came down, saw that Hallstein had been killed, and at once killed the slave. He went home and told his mother the news as she was sitting by the fire with her women.

A little later it was rumoured by the servants at Vidivellir that Droplaug, Helgi and the slave had had a long conversation the day Hallstein was killed; that slaying was not popular. Helgi Asbjarnarson took up the suit and summoned Droplaug and Helgi for plotting against Hallstein's life, and he prepared the suit for the Althing. Helgi Droplaugarson's case was not popular, and no one wanted to support him except Thorkel Geitisson and Ketil Thidrandason.

When men were leaving home for the Althing, Droplaug took the goods she and Hallstein had owned and, with her three-year-old son Herjolf, embarked on a ship in Berufiord. They left the

---

[1] 100 ounces of silver or that weight in money.

country and came to the Faeroes; there she bought herself land and lived till old age, and so she is out of the story.

VIII

Helgi Asbjarnarson conducted the case because the Hallsteinssons were out of the country. He now had a great following at the Althing. An attempt was made to reconcile the namesakes, but all that happened was that Helgi Asbjarnarson had his way. These were the terms: that for the slaying of Hallstein's twelve 'hundreds', each of the value of five cows were to be paid. [1] Helgi Droplaugarson was to go abroad for three years, and must not stay anywhere for more than one night before going away. If he did not go he would be as an outlaw to Helgi Asbjarnarson between Smjorvatnsheath and Lonsheath.

Helgi Droplaugarson made no move to go abroad. Then his brother Grim left his home to meet him, and they stayed the winter with Thorkel Geitisson in Krossavik and attended all the district Assemblies and meetings of men just as if Helgi had not been outlawed. Afterwards Hallstein's sons came out to Reydarfiord but Eindridi had died before they got back to Iceland. Thorod and Thorkel gave Helgi Asbjarnarson timber for a hall to reward him for taking action on behalf of their father.

That hall is still standing at Mjovaness.

Thorgrim Furcap was living at Midboer in Nordrfiord. His wife was Rannveig Bresting, the sister of Thordis who was married to Thorstein and related to Helgi Droplaugarson. In the spring at the Mula Assembly she asked her kinsman Helgi to come and make a division of property between herself and her husband, and the outcome was that he promised to come.

Some years before, at the Autumn Assembly, the Helgis had met at Thinghofdi. Helgi Droplaugarson had then to announce the law business, and he made a mistake at which people laughed a lot, and Helgi Asbjarnarson smiled. Helgi Droplaugarson saw that and said, 'I see Hrafnkel standing behind you, Helgi.'

'You needn't throw that in my teeth, Helgi,' said Helgi

---

[1] A 'hundred' means 120 ounces of silver, which varied in value.

Asbjarnarson. 'I'm warning you that next time we meet, only one of us will get away alive.'

Helgi Droplaugarson answered, 'Your threats may be terrible but they don't scare me. I count on piling up stones over your head at that meeting.' And that ended their talk for the time being.

IX

The next spring Flosi sent word from Svinafell to Thorkel Geitisson to come south, and bring a big crowd of men with him; Flosi wished to outlaw Arnor Orolfsson the brother of Halldor of the Woods whom Flosi had had killed. Thorkel mustered a band of thirty men and asked Helgi Droplaugarson to join him. Helgi answered, 'I'd be duty bound to come on that journey but I am ill, and shall stay at home.' Thorkel asked Grim to come, but he said he would not leave Helgi while he was ill. So then Thorkel went south to Svinafell with thirty men; from there Flosi went to Skogar with a hundred and twenty men.

A little later Helgi came to talk with his brother Grim, and said he wanted to go to their kinswoman Rannveig, and make the division of property between herself and Thorgrim Furcap. Thorkel and Gunnstein from Inner Krossavik went with them and two men of their household, so they were six in all. They went east over the heath and came to Thorkel at Torfastead; he had a daughter Tofa who was called Sun of the Mountainside and she was Helgi Droplaugarson's mistress. They stayed there that night, and Helgi and Tofa talked long together. She had a premonition that he might not come back from this expedition, and she went along the way with them, weeping bitterly. Helgi took off his good belt and moreover a decorated knife, and gave them to her, and then they parted. He and the others went to a farm called Straum; a man called Helgi the Lean joined them there, so they were seven in all. They came to Groa at Eyvindara, and she welcomed them warmly.

Groa had a workman called Thorbjorn and he took good care of the weapons there. Helgi Droplaugarson asked him to see to his sword while he was down the fiord, and Thorbjorn fetched him another sword.

They went from there to Nordfiord, to Thorbjorn's kinsman
Thorstein. This man had married Thordis, the sister of Rannveig
who was married to Thorgrim Furcap. The day Helgi
Droplaugarson was there, Thorkel Black Poet, the brother of
Thorarin of Saudarfiord,[1] came down from the heath and one
man with him. They spent the night there and had a great deal of
talk with Helgi, and they swore friendship together. Helgi asked
Thorkel, 'Where do you mean to go when you leave here?'

He replied, 'Out to Bjorn at Ness, because this winter he sold
some of my linen cloth. I'll be there three nights.'

Then Helgi said, 'I should like us to go together up over the fell.'
Thorkel said he would willingly do that; so they all went together
to Midboer, and from there Thorkel went out to Ness.

Helgi knocked at the door at Midboer and Rannveig came to
open it. Helgi asked her, 'Do you still want to divide the property
between yourself and Thorgrim?'

'Indeed I do,' she said. Then she named witnesses for herself,
and declared herself separated from Thorgrim Furcap, and she
took all his clothes and flung them into a cess-pit. After that Helgi
and Rannveig went away because Helgi planned to fetch her
property later. They travelled into Fannardale for their dinner.

When they had gone Thorgrim sprang up and wrapped his
woollen bed-cover about him, for he had no clothes left, and he
ran to Hof; a prominent man called Thorarin Mouldgrub lived
there. Thorarin said, 'Why are you up so early, Thorgrim, and
rather scantily attired?' He replied that his wife had been taken
away, 'and I want to ask you for your help in this affair'.

Thorarin answered, 'First of all I'll give you some clothes, for
that's your greatest need.' Afterwards Thorgrim ate dinner there.
Then Thorarin said, 'I advise you to find Helgi Asbjarnarson and
call on him to take up your case. If he refuses, as I think he may,
ask him when he means to make good the words he spoke at the
Thinghofdi Autumn Assembly. If he doesn't respond then, try this
plan: tell him that Helgi Droplaugarson and six men with him will
be going up the fell in three day's time. Go to Helgi Asbjarnarson
late this evening, because he himself locks the doors every night in
Mjovaness.'

[1] Perhaps an old spelling for Seydarfiord.

They parted, and Thorgrim went on his way and arrived at Mjovaness that same evening. Helgi was sitting by the fire and Thorgrim told him his errand, explaining his difficulty, but he got not a word from Helgi.

Then Thorgrim said, 'Now I must tell you this, Helgi; you've reached the point where you can't protect any of your thingmen from Helgi Droplaugarson, either at meetings or Assemblies of men. You gave him your word at the Thinghofdi Assembly that you would not both leave your next meeting alive – what about that meeting now? Can you go on letting him get the better of you?'

Helgi Asbjarnarson said, 'Did you think of all this, or did someone else?'

He replied, 'Thorarin Mouldgrub suggested it to me.'

Then Helgi Asbjarnarson said, 'Thorgrim, you must go up over the ridge on Myrar to Bjorn the White and tell him to come over here before midday tomorrow; then go back round Bolungarvoll and then to Vidivellir to meet the Hallsteinssons, and tell them to come here if they want to avenge their father. Then you must go down to the west of the lake below Ass to Ozur and tell him to come here, and then come back with him.'

Thorgrim went off at once, and during the day the men Helgi had sent for came to Mjovaness. There were two Norwegians staying with Helgi: one called Sigurd Cormorant and the other Onund. Then they left the house sixteen together to go to Hofdi. Helgi asked Hjarrandi and his brother Kari to go with him. Hjarrandi said, 'I'd have been ready if you'd asked me sooner.' Then eighteen together they went to Knutusel in Eyvindardale and lay in ambush for Helgi Droplaugarson. There was a man called Igul who had a son called Thord: they lived under Skagafell in Eyvindardale. From there they were to keep a look-out for movements of men, because they could see Helgi Droplaugarson's band before Helgi Asbjarnarson could.

X

Now we must return to where Thorkel Black Poet was coming to Fannardale to join Helgi Droplaugarson; he and his men stayed there that night. Helgi slept badly and woke up three times during the night. Thorkel asked him what he was dreaming, but Helgi wouldn't tell him; then they got dressed. Helgi asked Thorstein to look after Rannveig's affairs; 'I should like you to have her taken to my brother Grim's house.'

Before daybreak they left Fannardale and went up on to the heath, nine men together, and when they had climbed the slope Helgi lay down to rest on his cloak, as he had been finding it hard going. Then he scratched his cheek and rubbed his chin and said, 'I don't think there'll be much to scratch there by the time evening comes, but do you want to hear my dream, Thorkel, as much as you did last night?'

He answered, 'I want to just as much as I did then.'

'It seemed to me,' said Helgi, 'as if we were going along the way we are now, down from Eyvindardale to Kalfshval, and that eighteen or twenty wolves ran at us, and one was much larger than the rest. We wanted to get to the hillock which is in the valley but couldn't reach it; they attacked us at once and one clawed at my teeth and my chin. Then I woke up.'

Thorkel said, 'It must mean that men are lying in wait for you; they will be Helgi Asbjarnarson and other men of the neighbourhood. Most people here are getting tired of your riding roughshod over them. Now we have offered each other friendship, and I want you to come home with me and stay there for a while.'

Helgi answered, 'I must go on as I've planned.'

Then they went down from Eyvindardale and came to Thordis' farm; she was old, and both ugly and swarthy. Helgi was going to ask her for news, when just at that moment one of his men picked up snow, and made a snowball hard in his hand; he flung it at Thordis' cheek. It hurt her, and she said, 'The trolls take you all!'

Then Helgi said, 'It is shameful to strike a woman, and ill luck is home-bred.' Helgi got no news there.

Then they went away down to the river Valagil, and Thorkel Black Poet offered to go to Eyvindara with Helgi.

'There's no need for you to do that,' said Helgi, and so they parted. But when Thorkel had gone a little way up the slope he turned back to Helgi, who welcomed him and said he was showing himself a true friend. Then they went towards the gravel banks by Kalfsvad, and when they saw eighteen men running towards them Helgi Droplaugarson and his men turned for the hillock but could not reach it. Then they turned off the track and followed the edge of the gully beside the river Eyrargil; there was a little rise in the ground and the lower part was covered with a snowdrift, but nowadays that heath is all overgrown with brushwood, and there is a little cairn of stones where they fought.

Then Helgi asked his brother Grim whether he would aim his spear high or low at Helgi Asbjarnarson, and Grim chose high.

'You don't want my namesake killed, then,' said Helgi; 'his shield will be no shelter where I shall throw at him.'

Now they both flung spears at Helgi Asbjarnarson at the same moment, and Grim's went through the shield, and Helgi was not wounded by it. But Helgi Droplaugarson shot his at the kneecap, and it glanced down the leg splitting it open down to the instep, so that Helgi Asbjarnarson was put out of action at once. Then Bjorn the White sat down under Helgi's shoulders, and neither of them fought any more that day. Ozur from Ass turned away, saying he would not fight against Helgi Droplaugarson, and he sat down to one side. Thord Cormorant was keeping look-out for Helgi Asbjarnarson, but had fallen into the river and his clothes were frozen. He thought he had a bone to pick with Helgi Droplaugarson and plunged into the snowdrift to attack him, but when he got into it Helgi flung a spear between his legs through the scrotum; he fell on his back with the spear sticking fast in the snow, and he was pinned there in the drift all day.

After that Helgi Asbjarnarson egged his kinsmen on to fight, calling on Hjarrandi by name. Then Hjarrandi and Kari set on Helgi Droplaugarson, while the Hallsteinssons and another man went for Grim. Thorkel Black Poet was attacked by two Norwegians. He fell then, but he had killed one of the Norwegians; Sigurd, who was the third best fighting man in Helgi Asbjarnarson's following, was badly wounded, because Thorkel was the best warrior in the Droplaugarsons' band.

Now they went hard at it, but when Hjarrandi and Kari were both attacking Helgi Droplaugarson, Helgi the Lean from Straum sprang at Kari. They fought for a time and Kari fell, but Helgi the Lean was badly wounded. Then Hjarrandi made a fierce onslaught on Helgi Droplaugarson and struck at him time and again; Helgi struck no fewer or lighter blows, but the sword he was using was worthless.

Helgi spoke to Hjarrandi, 'You would have pressed on harder if you had married Helgi Asbjarnarson's free-born daughter.'[1]

Hjarrandi replied, 'Whatever you say they are both of them Helgi's daughters,' and then, in spite of Helgi's taunts, he fought on more fiercely than ever.

Helgi's shield was much hacked about; he saw that it wouldn't be much more use to him as it was. Then he showed his fighting skill by flinging his sword and shield into the air and, catching his sword in his left hand, he struck at Hjarrandi and hit him on the thigh; the sword didn't bite the bone but glanced off it down to the hollow of the knee, and that wound put him out of action. Just at that moment Hjarrandi struck at Helgi, but he warded off the blow with his shield, and Hjarrandi's sword jerked into his face, striking his teeth and cutting his lower lip. Then Helgi said, 'I was never good-looking, and this hasn't improved me much.' Then he grasped his beard in his hand, thrust it into his mouth and bit on it; Hjarrandi lurched into the snowdrift and sat down. People say that their encounter would not have lasted so long if Helgi had had his own sword, and had not had to face so many, yet Hjarrandi was a very brave man.

Then Helgi saw that his brother Grim had fallen, but all who had attacked him were dead; Grim himself was wounded to death. Helgi took Grim's sword from him and said, 'Now the man I thought the best has fallen – well, my namesake won't want this to be our parting,' and he made for where Helgi Asbjarnarson was sitting. All the men had fled from the snowdrift and no one was waiting for Helgi.

'There you stand, Ozur,' he said, 'and I've no need to beware of you because you were the one who sprinkled me with water.'[2] And as he was going down towards Ozur, Ozur was quick to act, and seeing the life of one or other of the Helgis was at stake, he made up his mind to run Helgi Droplaugarson through, and

[1] See note on page 79.
[2] The custom of sprinkling children with water when they were given a name may have been practised in the north before Christianity was introduced there.

lunged at him with his spear; Helgi forced himself on to it, saying to Ozur, 'Now you've betrayed me.'

Ozur saw that Helgi had turned towards him and might reach him with his sword, so all at once he thrust the spear with Helgi on it away from him. It twisted down into the ground and then he let go of it. When Helgi saw that he could not reach Ozur, he said, 'I was slow just then, but you were quick.' He staggered back into the snow, and so ended the life of Helgi Droplaugarson. Five of Helgi Asbjarnarson's men were killed, and all the others were wounded except Bjorn the White and Ozur. Thorkel Black Poet and his companion fell with Helgi Droplaugarson, and also a Norwegian who had come with Helgi from his home and Grim, Helgi's brother.

XI

Helgi Asbjarnarson rode away from the battle propped up on horseback; Hjarrandi rode alone, but Kari was carried home to Hofdi on a shield, and a mound was heaped over him there. When they came to Hofdi they were asked for news, and they told what had happened.

Then a man asked, 'What did Helgi Droplaugarson do more than other men today?'

Sigurd Cormorant answered, 'If all those with Helgi had been like him, not one of us would have escaped.'

Helgi the Lean came to Eyvindara and told Groa the news; he was badly wounded. Then Groa spoke to her son Bard; 'Get horses and draught-horses and we will go and fetch Helgi and Grim.' They did so and came to the battlefield; they rolled the brothers on to a sledge and Thorkel with them. Those who were wounded rode on horseback, and the others who were dead were buried there. Then they set off towards home, and Groa kept closest to the sledge Grim was on and had him driven gently. They came home and had the bodies carried into an outhouse, and Groa said, 'Now my son Bard and I will wake over the bodies but you stay with the living and give them hospitality.' And when men were asleep Groa crossed over the water to Ekkjufell where Alfgerd the doctor lived. Groa asked her to come home with her,

letting her know what had happened. When they reached
Eyvindara Grim was still alive; Alfgerd bound up his wounds and
took him away with her. The next morning a mound was raised at
the south end of the house by the river Eyvind, and Bard took the
bodies there, and with him was a man they were most confident
would keep the secret of Grim's still being alive; and Helgi and
Thorkel were buried there.

Grim lay wounded that winter and so did Helgi Asbjarnarson.
Now it was rumoured that Grim was still alive, some confirming
this, and others saying it was a lie; the rumour sprang up first in
Groa's household. Then Helgi, when he heard that Grim had not
died, had a closet-bed made in Mjovaness. After a time Grim went
north to Krossavik to Thorkel Geitisson and was given a good
welcome there.

XII

Helgi Asbjarnarson bought land to the north-east at a place called
Eidar, and sold Mjovaness. He thought he would be better off
there with his thingmen[1] round him, and he had a closet-bed made
there. His wife Thordis asked him why he chose to live on land
which was wooded right up to the buildings, so that no one could
see men on the move even if they came quite close up to the farm.
Then Helgi spoke this verse:

'When dusk begins to fall –
I have many forebodings in the wood –
I'm making a verse in silence –
That foes prepared for battle attack me with weapons.'

Grim stayed some years in Krossavik and was never cheerful;
he never laughed after Helgi was killed.

On one occasion Thorkel Geitisson had to make a journey into
Eyjafiord to settle a dispute among his thingmen. He rode away
from home but Grim stayed behind, occupying himself with the
farm. Some nights later Grim got ready to leave home, saying he
had to collect some money from a man called Thorgrim who lived
in Hjardarhagi in Jokulsdale. 'It's now clear to me that he's not
going to pay,' said Grim.

[1] A chieftain's followers and members of an assembly.

Then Jorunn, Thorkel's wife, the daughter of Einar from Thvera, said, 'I'll pay you this debt; and don't you go on any account.'

'He would still owe me the money,' said Grim, and he took some provisions and left home; his foster-brothers Glum and Thorkel Crane went with him. They journeyed till they came to a farm called Ranga, west of the lake; Grim and Glum swam over supporting Thorkel Crane, and they came to a farm called Bakki, east of the lake. They went into the cowshed there and took a spade and shovel; afterwards they went to Oddmar's brook west of Eid[ar] Wood. There they dug an underground room for themselves, throwing all the earth away into the brook; they wanted a hide-out in case of need.

XIII

That day, when they were by the brook, people were riding away from the Lambaness Assembly, and many men were on their way to Eid[ar] with Helgi Asbjarnarson. There was a man called Ketilorm who lived at Hrollaugsstead; he travelled with Helgi, and thirty men with him; so did Helgi's sons-in-law Bjorn and Hjarrandi.

That evening Grim and his men left the underground room, came up to Eid[ar] and went in through the door of the cowshed from which a covered way led into the main building. They stood there, and saw what was going on in the farmhouse.

In the evening Helgi Asbjarnarson said to his wife, 'Where do you mean to sleep Ketilorm and his wife?'

She answered, 'I've made a good bed for them near the door.'

Helgi said, 'They are to lie in our bed, because they always move out of theirs every time we sleep with them.'

Thordis replied, 'You're not always as much on your guard as you should be. If I were Grim I should plan to attack you when you had many guests and much to look after.'

He answered, 'It's often thrown in my teeth that I am over cautious.' Then he and not Thordis decided the matter of the beds.

Now Grim said to Thorkel Crane, 'Go inside and try to get hold of my brother Helgi's sword – the one Thorbjorn sharpened.'

Thorkel went in, and came back with the sword. Later Grim said, 'Go in again, and try to find out where Helgi Asbjarnarson and his wife are sleeping.' Thorkel was only away a short time, and he told Grim that they were sleeping in a closet- bed with no shutters near the door.

There was a man called Arnod, and he was blind; he was one of Helgi Asbjarnarson's household and very strong. He was lying over against Helgi on the platform by a partition.

Then Grim said to Thorkel, 'I want you to go in and attack Helgi Asbjarnarson, because you are the man next after myself most bound to avenge my brother Helgi.'[1]

'That's true,' said Thorkel.

Then Grim put the sword into Thorkel's hand and they walked right up to the main door. Thorkel stopped and spoke to Grim: 'I don't want you to imagine that I'm afraid of going in to Helgi, but it seems strange that you ask me, because you used to say that you would not allow anyone to avenge your brother but yourself.'

Grim replied, 'It's because I never dreamed that my brother Helgi would need vengeance while I was alive.'

Thorkel then made to go in, but Grim caught hold of him and said, 'You're a fine fellow, Thorkel, but I don't think you're likely to give Helgi as deep a wound as I want. So let it be as you said. I will not allow anyone else to avenge Helgi.' Then Grim grasped the sword and said, 'Thorkel, you are to hold on to the door ring because I know I can trust you not to panic; Glum is to shoot the bolt across the door.'

Before Grim went in he took a short heavy cudgel in his hand; he was wearing a tunic and linen breeks and had no shoes on his feet. He walked into the room and saw there was a pile of logs by the door that opened into the cowshed; earlier that evening Glum had tied all the cows in the shed together by their tails. Then Grim went into the closet-bed next to the bed of Helgi and his wife. There he put down the cudgel he was carrying, and then went to Helgi's bed and pulled the bed-clothes off Helgi. Helgi woke up and said, 'Did you touch me, Thordis? But why is your hand so cold?'

---

[1] Thorkel, as foster-brother of Grim and Helgi, had an obligation to avenge them.

'I didn't touch you,' she said, 'but you are not on the alert and I'm afraid something terrible may happen.' After that they fell asleep.

Then Grim went up to Helgi and moved away Thordis' hand which she had laid over him, and said, 'Wake up, Helgi, you've had your sleep out!' Then Grim ran Helgi through with his sword. Helgi cried out 'Wake up! I'm attacked! Out of your beds, boys!'

Grim took the cudgel he had put down, and flung it at the pile of logs, toppling it to the ground. Then men in the room jumped up, thinking that the killer had run off in the direction of the noise, but Grim turned back towards the door he had come in by. Then a man seized Grim round the middle and hoisted him up on his chest; it was Arnod, and he called out, 'Here! Come here! I've got the villain!'

Then Grim said, 'Hands off, wretch! Let me go! I was trying to avenge Helgi.' Arnod felt him over with one hand and found he was barefoot and wearing linen breeks; he let Grim go, saying, 'I've let you go, but maybe I ought to have kept hold of you.' Then Grim sprang for the door and ran out; Thorkel shut it, and Glum shot the bolt, and they went to their underground room and found refuge there.

Then those left behind considered what to do. They decided to keep a watch on all the fords and to lie in wait by the bridge over the river Jokul. Hjarrandi and Ketilorm and Helgi's kinsmen-in-law were the first on the scene and set out on the search. When most of them returned home from it Helgi was still alive and asked if Bjorn and Hjarrandi had come back.

'Here I am,' said Bjorn.

'That's how it is, then,' said Helgi; 'Hjarrandi is still the one who's doing his utmost for me.' Then Helgi died.

Now night passed by and Grim and his companions left the underground room and went up along the lake to Hofdi where they saw a tent. Grim walked up to it and said, 'Why do you allow thieves so near your ship?' Thorlak was the owner of the ship, and he had come to it with some Norwegians. He lent Grim a boat and they rowed across the lake. Grim took the boat back, and afterwards swam over again. From there they followed along the lake to the river Jokul, and Grim swam over it with Thorkel

Crane and Glum did too. They travelled north to Krossavik and
Thorkel Geitisson had not yet come home; they were asked their
news and said they had none to tell.

The next day Grim was playing a boardgame with a Norwegian
when one of Thorkel and Jorunn's children bumped into the table
and upset the board. The Norwegian kicked the boy and he broke
wind. Grim burst out laughing. Then Jorunn went up to him and
asked, 'What has happened on your journey so that now you can
laugh? What news have you to tell?'

Then Grim spoke a verse:

> 2.   'Men laughed when Grim was wounded
>   Hurt in the south.
>   No one gained by that.
>   The seafaring man is whistling another way:
>   In the mountains around Lagarfljot:
>   I have heard that the chieftain is dead.'

'You've avenged your brother Helgi, haven't you?' said Jorunn.
Then Grim spoke another verse:[1]

> 3. 'Now I've utterly avenged the slaying of Helgi
>   On the warrior, and I rejoice at that.
>   The sword struck home: I killed the open-handed man.
>   Now warlike Bjarni will have to avenge his kinsman.'
>
> (Now I think I've avenged somewhat
> the strife of nails [battle] sufficiently
> Helgi's slaying and laughs
> my mind at that, on him who performs, [man]
> now is to war-eager Bjarni,
> bit edge on raven's gladdener [fighting man],
> of arm-fire [gold] I killed the spender,
> matter kinsman to avenge.)

'The fact is', said Jorunn, 'that we are without a protector since
my man is not at home. Yet we would have run the risk of

---

[1] This verse about the killing of Helgi Asbjarnarson is the only one that really fits
its context. Verses 4 and 5 are about the battle at Eyvindardale and refer to the fall
of Helgi Droplaugarson. Verse 6 is ascribed to some unknown sailor.

harbouring you had we not been neighbours of Bjarni, Helgi
Asbjarnarson's kinsman.'

Grim and his companions lay there in hiding until Thorkel
came home. When he arrived he went to see Grim and asked for
his news, and how the killing of Helgi had come about. Grim told
him how it had gone, and spoke these verses:

4. 'Helgi's well-known sharp-edged sword struck men:
   It slashed a man's leg
   When spear-points pierced the breasts of men
   In the battle.

5. 'Helgi performed great deeds among warriors in battle:
   The sword clanged when men fell.
   Men far and wide heard of this
   When he, glad to give the raven bread, wounded three in
      battle.'

   (Helgi performed among warriors,
   the sword clanged in the slain-fall [battle]
   far and wide that could people,
   freemen's work [great deeds] in the tumult, hear of
   when he who rated highly the noise of the battle-plain
      [fighting man] made
   at the fight of Gondul's [valkyrie] path [battlefield],
   glad in Hild's [valkyrie] weather [combat]
   raven's servant [warrior] three of wounded.)

6. 'I had to be out at dawn
   Four days in fear
   After I the keen warrior won the fight,
   Let the blood-stained sword pierce the open-handed man.'

   (The man who drives a ship fast had outside
   the wave-horse [ship] to lie
   four periods of twelve hours in fear
   formerly, after I won the battle,
   when [I] the son of Thor [man] of attack
   keen, let, of swords
   swift, on the decreaser of gold [man]
   wound-wand [sword] stained with blood stand.)

Then Thorkel rode to the Althing, but Grim and his companions stayed in a tent on the mountainside called Snowfell up above Krossavik.

XIV

Helgi Asbjarnarson's nephew Hrafnkel the Godi brought a suit for a killing against Grim. Thorkel Geitisson offered money compensation on Grim's behalf, but Hrafnkel would not accept this, and Grim was outlawed. Then men went home from the Althing.

That summer a ship owned by Norwegians came to Krossavik, and the captain and three of his men took quarters with Thorkel. When autumn came Grim moved down the mountain to a ledge where the grass began; there was a big cairn above the tent and another below. The place has since been called Grim's House.

The Norwegians came to Krossavik for games and to meet their captain. One of them said, 'I think I see a tent, or else a grey rock up there on the fell, but I think it's a tent.'

Thorkel answered, 'You have very good eyesight; it is a rock, and we call it the Tent Rock.' They said no more just then.

The next night Thorkel went to Grim and his companions and said, 'Men will soon be coming up the fell and I want you to go home to Arneidarstead. Ingjald your father-in-law is a wise man and will keep you in safety, but if he thinks it will be too awkward for him, then come back here.' So they went to Ingjald and took up their quarters in the cave now known as Grim's Cave. Ingjald said to his shepherd, 'Say nothing about it if some of our sheep go missing.' Later on a woman house servant said to Ingjald, 'Our brook has got so dirty that we can hardly drink the water.'

'That's because it was blocked,' he said. 'but I've been to clear it.' But in point of fact Grim was digging an underground room and it opened into his wife's bed where he lay at night, and the earth had been carried into the brook.

Thorkel the Wise lived at Njardvik: he was a near kinsman of Grim's and was endowed with second sight. He was very much on his own. Godi Hrafnkel gave him a hundred[1] of silver to find out

---

[1] 120 ounces.

where Grim had gone to earth. Thorkel journeyed over the fell into the open country upstream from the east and downstream to the west; then he arrived at Arneidarstead.

Grim had a six-year-old son; Thorkel met the boy and asked him, 'Are you Grim's son?'

'I am,' said the boy.

'Is your father at home?' asked Thorkel.

'I don't know, but I wouldn't say if I did.'

In the evening a woman asked, 'Where is Grim's bucket? I can't find it.'

'What's out of the way about Grim's bucket?' cut in Thorkel.

At that Ingjald spoke up and said, 'The women call our goat Grim and they give him water in that bucket.' Then Thorkel suspected that Grim was there, and he went away and told Hrafnkel how matters stood.

In the spring Ingjald and Thorkel Crane left home, taking the higher route going south down the glacier and coming down to Hornafiord where a ship was laid up. Ingjald took a passage in it for Grim and all his company including Thorkel Crane, and he gave the captain money to keep quiet about this; Grim and his wife were to come there in secret. Afterwards Ingjald went home and a little later he took Grim and his companions to the ship without anyone getting to know, and he stayed by the ship till they put out to sea; then he went home. Hrafnkel got to know that Ingjald had helped Grim, and fined him three marks of silver for this.

Grim and his company sailed into Sognfiord. Then Captain Thorkel said to Grim, 'I won't refuse you food, but I can't undertake to protect you from Gunnar the Norwegian[1] or any of those who wish you dead.' Then Thorkel bought horses for Grim and his company and got them a guide to Opland,[2] and he and Grim parted in friendship.

Then Grim and his wife journeyed till they came to the house of a man called Finngeir: he was a young man and well off for money. His sister was called Sigrid and she was a beautiful woman and well skilled in many things. Grim and his wife stayed

[1] See *The Fljotsdale Saga*, Chapters XVII–XXII.

[2] The story of Grim's journey to Opland and fight with Gaus is purely legendary.

there for the night, and Finngeir asked Grim, 'Where are you travelling to?' Grim told him how things were with him.

Finngeir said, 'Stay here for a fortnight if you want to.' When that time was up Finngeir said, 'You can go to the house that used to be my brother's, and your company with you, and if you want to stay there, Grim, treat it as your own.' Grim took that offer.

XV

Gaus was a (berserk) viking, one of a band of four, and they were hard to deal with. They brought great dishonour on many people; iron would hardly cut them. Gaus had been some years in Opland and had driven two farmers from their homesteads and settled himself there afterwards. Later Gaus asked for Finngeir's sister Fridgerd[1] but she would not marry him. Then Gaus challenged Finngeir to a duel.

Finngeir answered, 'If I were four years older I would not hesitate, but still, I would rather fight with you than marry my sister to you.'

Finngeir offered men money to fight with Gaus, and his sister to the one who killed him; but no one would undertake this.

Grim went with Finngeir to the duelling island and offered to fight in his stead. Then Gaus came there with his men, and put down a stake of six marks of silver[2] for the duel. 'I'll take that money,' said Grim.

Grim had two swords because Gaus could blunt blades. Grim fought equally well with either hand; he brandished one sword in his left hand and struck at Gaus with the right, cutting off his leg above the knee. Gaus fell, and at that moment he swung his sword at Grim and slashed Grim's leg, wounding him to the bone. Then the viking fled away and Grim got the silver and much renown for his deed. Finngeir gave Grim the farm he had been looking after, together with all the property, land and stock.

Grim's wound became poisoned and his leg swelled up. One

---

[1] In the previous chapter called Sigrid.
[2] 48 ounces of silver, 1 mark equals 8 ounces.

evening a woman came there who said she was a doctor; she asked
to bind up Grim's wound, and she did so, and disappeared. A little
later Grim's leg became swollen all the way up to his belly. They
sent for a priest and Grim took the sacrament,[1] and afterwards
died. That woman was called Gefjon; she had been Gaus' mistress
and was skilled in magic.

A year went by, and in the spring Finngeir bought a ship for
Helga, and she sailed for Iceland with all her property; Thorkel
Crane sailed with her and they made Reydarfiord. Ingjald went to
meet his daughter and took her home to Arneidarstead, and she
stayed there ever after. Helga gave Thorkel half the ship, and sold
the other half to the Norwegians. Thorkel went abroad the
following spring, and this is the end of his story.

Thordis, who had been married to Helgi Asbjarnarson, was
given to Hoskuld the son of Thorgeir the Godi of Ljosavatn.
Hoskuld took Glum, the man who was with Grim Droplaugarson
when Helgi Asbjarnarson was killed, and he and Thordis had him
put to death. After Ingjald's death Helga [Grim's widow] lived on
at Arneidarstead with their son Thorkel. Thorvald had a son
Ingjald. His son was called Thorvald, who told this story. Helgi
Droplaugarson fell the year after Thangbrand came to Iceland.[2]

---

[1] An anachronism.
[2] Icelandic annals give 998 for the battle of Eyvindardale. According to Ari,
Thangbrand came to Iceland in 997 or 998. He introduced Christianity to Iceland.

INDEX OF PERSONAL AND PLACE NAMES

N.B. Entries beginning with 'Th' appear at the end of the Index